SILENCER'S END

VOLUME ONE

DAVID L. LITVIN

SILENCER'S END

Copyright©2023. All rights reserved.

David L. Litvin

Cover Design by A Novel Idea Author Services.

This book is a work of fiction. The names, characters, places, and incidents are the products of the author's imagination or are used fictitiously. Any resemblance to actual events, business establishments, locales, or persons, living or dead, is entirely coincidental.

All rights reserved. No part of this publication may be reproduced, stored in a retrieval system, or transmitted in any form or by any means (electronic, mechanical, photocopying, recording, or otherwise) without the prior written permission of both the copyright owner and the publisher. The only exception is brief quotations in printed reviews.

The scanning, uploading, and distribution of this book via the Internet or via any other means without the permission of the publisher is illegal and punishable by law. Please purchase only authorized electronic editions, and do not participate in or encourage electronic piracy of copyrighted materials.

Your support of the author's rights is appreciated.

Published in the United States of America by:

David L. Latvin

www.davidlitvin.com

ONE

There has been a lot of disagreement lately about what it means to be a psychopath, or more recently, a sociopath. Generally, it's a person with no remorse, often narcissistic, and for the most part a dangerous asshole. There is even more recent research that suggests it is surprisingly common. That there are a great number of sociopaths in our midst, a lot more than previously known, yet most somehow at least appear to function normally. I am most definitely not one of those.

Oh, I am a sociopath, no doubt. But I do have a very strong sense of right or wrong, not unlike a normal person. I can't "feel" right versus wrong. But I can see it, play with it, and understand it. At least intellectually. The big difference being that I can act on my impulses without guilt. Especially when I see injustice, or at least what I believe to be injustice. But it is exactly this strong sense of right and wrong that has led me to this rather ignominious end. I'm in jail, a tiny and wretched one to be sure, but most certainly a jail, somewhere on the extreme outskirts of that bustling metropolis known as Bentonville, Arkansas.

It is a very small town whose name I don't even know. It has just one car and two officers that, for all I know, are volunteers. Their "jail" consists of just two cells and a big desk, all in one room. The cells themselves are almost comically ancient. They are two attached steel cages with old-school steel keys and locks.

And here I sit. Waiting until tomorrow morning for some CIA officials to take me into custody, presumably to try and figure out who I am. The cops that arrested me didn't seem to have any particular interest. They hadn't even bothered to "book" me or even ask me for my ID. I take no pride in knowing this will be big news when they do finally figure it out. "The Silencer," as I have come to be known on social media, has been caught and will soon be unmasked. Not that I wear a physical mask, nor have I ever spent more than a moment on social media unless I needed to, but you get the point.

I guess now is as good a time as any to explain why many millions of people will care. Some will be thrilled to have a very dangerous killer off the street. But an equal, if not greater number, will not like that my peculiar form of justice has come to an end—at least from me. But it won't really "end" at all because I am far from being the only one. There will be a replacement for me, and my guess is that they will be smart enough not to become famous.

"Attention-seeking behavior." It's a phrase that has snuck into our collective consciousness through a combination of current trends in psychotherapy and social media. It is a popular belief, and quite likely a correct one, that it is human nature to seek attention. I agree. And it's probably never been truer than it is now. All of us are awash in sensory input pretty much all of the time. Much of it is voluntary. Television, radio, social media, online videos, and the like. And so much of this media is truly great. I could argue that we live in the golden age of media, especially television. The sheer volume of television programming almost demands that a certain amount of it is great. And it is. There is something for every taste, every sensibility.

But a lot of it is forced on us. Billboards, ads, clickbait, commercials, and writing on the bathroom wall. Everything is seeking our attention while almost nothing returns the favor. Almost nothing gives us the attention we all crave. And so we starve. In a loud world with the volume growing ever louder, we are alone and desperate for attention of almost any kind— good or bad. We delight in the smallest hit of dopamine we get from our likes and retweets. Anyone could argue that this record of my acts is in itself a cry for attention, though certainly not in any conventional sense. Obviously, I'm not using my real name. So, any attention this gets won't celebrate or defame me personally. But it is a confession to some twenty-five murders or more. And there is a pretty good chance that I will live long enough to know if anyone reads it. So yes, this is almost certainly "attention-seeking behavior." I will have to tell that to my therapist if I ever get another one. As I will soon wind up in the legal system, they will almost certainly assign me one.

So not all attention-seeking behavior is bad. After all most of the good things that society has produced have come from people looking for attention in the form of money, fame, and power. There's nothing wrong with that in theory. But there's plenty of attention seeking for its own sake and, for lack of a better word, that's what pisses me off. That particular method of attention seeking produces nothing good. And the bad it produces ranges from slight nuisance to genuine danger and disruption.

Consider for a moment the person who deliberately tunes their vehicles to make very loud obnoxious noises. Everywhere they go they deliver, at the very least, slight discomfort to everyone around them. Why? Who would want to be the person that causes discomfort, even a minor one, to everyone in their path? Even I wouldn't do that. What's the point?

The answer, unfortunately, is quite a few people. People so desperate for any form of attention that they are willing to harm everyone around them, if only slightly. I will argue until my last breath that the world is a better place without these assholes. And I have dispatched some myself. These were my first. They happened to catch her attention from an article that pondered the question if it was some form of organized terror attack. Albeit a fairly subtle one. I would argue that it doesn't matter. A lot of people were being harmed. Now they are not. The reasons matter less than the result.

Not too long ago there were at least four, and maybe more people, who were riding the streets of Manhattan on finely tuned motorbikes. They were tuned specifically to make noise, and make noise they did. There was a great deal of media coverage of the situation. One of the articles suggested that almost a million people were being kept awake by those bikes, screaming around the otherwise empty Manhattan streets between 2 and 5 a.m. The police, for their part, had made an effort. They caught and ticketed the perpetrators more than a dozen times and made but one arrest for "malicious mischief." Legally, there wasn't much more they could have done. So what they called the "buzzing" of Manhattan did not stop.

I stopped it.

With two very small pieces of lead. Rather two copper-and-alloy composite bullets with a small amount of lead. It just sounds more dramatic to say lead. Each of these bullets passed through the side of the neck of a cyclist and out the other side. Each of them was declared dead from the ensuing crash of their bikes. But they would have died of the wounds even if they had survived the wrecks. The police and official coroner reports never officially mentioned the bullet wounds. The bullets were never found. But the "buzzing" of Manhattan stopped. If there were others doing the same, they must have figured out that getting my attention probably wasn't good for them. Untold millions of Manhattanites were spared the torture of sleeplessness.

You're welcome.

TWO

That was the first time I killed anybody. Though it was definitely not the first time I had seriously thought about killing anyone. At that point, I had spent almost a year preparing for exactly that. But in my admittedly abnormal mind, it was an almost mathematical equation. Would the world be a better or worse place if these dick bags were permitted to continue to exist. To continue harming the innocent?

By the way, there are no delusions at work here, religious or otherwise. I am a sociopath but not a schizophrenic. Schizophrenics are often extremely religious and may kill thinking they are the hand of God. Preferably not the hand he jerks off with. I, on the other hand, was acting in a strictly practical manner. A perfect example of "doing well by doing good."

And I got paid. But I can explain that later.

The skills I used to execute the project were nothing particularly special either. I have no military background, but my father did. I spent much of my youth with high-powered, long-distance weapons. My father, an Army sniper, was never much for hobbies or recreation. But he did have an interest in me. His only son. Shooting accurately was the only thing he knew or cared about. And so we did it together, a lot, even after his military career ended. We didn't kill anybody, of course. We didn't even kill anything. He had no interest in hunting. If you forced me to say what he was interested in, I would have to say it was a single thing: precision. He loved the precision of hitting something almost half a mile away with what amounts to a tool. This is how we bonded. The only way he knew how. Which was just fine for me. From a little boy and well into my twenties, I was happy to shoot with him. We didn't talk a whole lot. If I shared with him a childhood or a teenage problem I had, he would always answer. But, of course, the answers themselves would be short, precise. He loved me, a feeling I have never experienced firsthand. And this was his way of showing it. It was more than enough.

I have a mother as well. A loving and doting one at that. I am their only child. Apparently, she had suffered some kind of complication during my birth that rendered her incapable of conceiving again. If she suffered any emotional damage, which she surely must have, it was never spoken of or revealed to me. She was and is a wonderful mother to me. If I am a monster, as many will surely see me, it is definitely not because of my parents.

Being a military family, we moved around a lot. My father was deployed overseas at least twice that I can remember. The first time was for about eighteen months. I was eight when he got home. For a time, he felt like a stranger, I think to us both. And he seemed different. I don't trust the recollections of an eight-year-old sociopath, but I do trust my mom. And she was also sure that the man who came back that time was a different man. It wasn't hard to figure out why. It had been the first time his magnificent shooting skills had been used to kill. There wasn't a dramatic transformation. It was more like weariness. He just seemed tired. In time he returned to normal. Or we simply got used to who he'd become. But I could tell. He experienced guilt. Something I could never know. He was deployed once more after that for almost a year. But that time he returned the same man as when he had left. Whatever damage may have been done was done. He retired from the military as soon as he reached full benefits. Still a young man and still with the passion for shooting and precision.

So as much fun as it might be to see me as the aberrational result of an abusive and tortured upbringing. Nope. They were cool. Still are.

A better theory of who I have become might have something to do with my relationships with people outside of my nuclear family. Ours was a small family. All my grandparents, except one, passed before I was seven, so I have almost no memory of them. I have a few stray aunts, uncles, and cousins but none that were ever particularly close to me or my parents, either emotionally or geographically. With one notable exception. And since we moved around a lot, I developed a habit of making shallow friendships. A habit that has continued into adulthood. It might be fair to say that I am friendly but without friends. It just never seemed sensible to develop deep bonds when my earliest memories were of being uprooted. It's nobody's fault, it's just military life and not at all uncommon among people raised in a military family. And even more so in a sociopath.

So, in this instance it's hard to see where the normal ends and the crazy starts. I think my parents knew I was not normal pretty early on. Even as an infant, toddler, and child I did not cry very much. And even then, only as the result of direct, apparent physical pain. I was pretty good natured. As I said, I made friends pretty easily. I just didn't react to sadness or emotional situations like everyone else did. But I did learn to simulate those behaviors early on. I can remember when my mother's father passed away, I was about twelve. I knew this was a big deal and acted—"acted" being the keyword—appropriately. But even as I perfected this craft, I don't think I fooled my parents.

As for my relations with the fairer sex. Well, they have also been frequent and shallow as well. I'm straight, and I am definitely appreciative of a beautiful woman. But I suspect that my attraction to beauty is different than it is in so-called "normal" people. I have a sex drive, but until recently it was sporadic, situational, and almost mechanical. It's as if I perceived sexual desire and beauty as something to be examined and studied. I don't so much "feel" it. It's more of a combination of expectations and curiosity. Some part of me still wants to be like everyone else, so I understand the allure of having a beautiful woman on my arm, in my bed, in my life. But the pursuit, until recently, has been hollow and more like a hobby. I am not capable of the "love" and affection that a woman—any woman —deserves from a mate. I can pretend with the best of them. But my few "significant others" over the years have not been fooled. Nor did I try to fool them. If I ever found one that would be satisfied with what I'm capable of giving I may even settle down some day. But from this jail cell, that scenario is a bit difficult to picture.

School was always a bore. I do like to learn, and I am pretty good at it. But beyond the basics of reading, writing, and arithmetic, I preferred my own slate of subjects, especially psychology. For a time in my teens, it became almost an obsession to learn enough to determine exactly what the fuck was wrong with me. But my interests soon blossomed into an honest desire to learn about the world outside of myself. But much like my relationships with people, my interests were very wide, but shallow. Once I would grasp the overriding theme of what I was learning, I would lose interest and move on to something else. It comes in handy. I can hold a decent conversation with almost anyone about almost anything. As the saying goes, "I know a little about a lot, and a lot about nothing." The only thing I was expert at was shooting. And only that particular type of shooting that my dad had spent so many very pleasant hours patiently teaching me. But that would soon change.

When I graduated high school, there was no discussion at all about me attending college. I simply wasn't interested. It's not that I didn't want to learn. I was still a voracious reader of almost exclusively nonfiction and even textbooks on subjects that interested me at any particular time. Economics became a subject that I pursued far more deeply than most others. Probably because economics is, at least in my mind, very similar to psychology. Economic behavior and economic thought echo human behavior and thought. Almost as if the two social sciences run parallel to each other. In fact, when you really get down to it, economics, psychology, and even philosophy are really one science. As for my own economy, I think my parents expected me to join the Army as my dad had done. But they put no pressure on me to do so. I considered it. With my skills and decent grades, I would have been warmly embraced by the recruiters, one of whom my dad brought home to meet me. I resisted and more or less played for time, taking jobs here and there to provide my own spending money. Around the time I turned twenty-five, my path, for better or worse, revealed itself.

THREE

My Aunt Jane is my father's sister and almost two years older than my dad. As children often do, I have always thought of her as being "old." But in reality, even now she is only fifty-five and could objectively pass for mid-forties. At least the last time I saw her. She is tall and narrow in the same way that both my father and I are. Besides my parents, she has been the only nearly constant person in my life. She never married, but I do recall her bringing an occasional boyfriend to family functions over the years. She was very much like a second mother to me—in some ways even more than my actual, perfectly acceptable mom. She always seemed enthralled by me and I got her constant attention as a child anytime she was around, which was pretty often considering how much we moved. She would come and visit, staying anywhere from just an evening to a week or more at a time. She would ask me questions about myself. School, friends, sports, nothing seemed too small for her. And of course, in my youth I was all too happy to tell her. An adult's full attention is intoxicating, even to a young sociopath. My parents could tell, but if there was any sense of competition, it was never apparent to me. I think my mom likes Jane and felt like she was glad to share her only son with a woman who had no children of her own. She was far and away my favorite aunt, and that seemed to suit everyone just fine. She wasn't a shooter. She never came with me and my dad on our almost daily quests to destroy inanimate objects from long distances. But we did talk, a lot. And as I got older, more and more of her auntly concern turned toward my love interests, my future, and my friendships.

It was some time just after my twenty-fifth birthday that she offered to take me to lunch, just the two of us. This was unusual in that our previous interactions were usually a part of family gatherings and never away from home. But it raised no suspicion in me. My favorite aunt just wanted to take her so-far-underachieving nephew to lunch. I expected a pep talk, and I got one. Just not the one I was expecting. She was blunt, as was often the case, but never quite this blunt.

"You don't feel a goddamned thing, do you?" she asked as I looked up from my burrito.

"What do you mean?" Was my immediate reply, even though I knew exactly what she meant.

"You don't feel guilt, remorse, love, sorrow, or any of the better-known emotions. You're like me, a blank slate. It must be genetics of some kind. Lucky us." And she laughed.

I stared at her from across the table for what seemed like forever but was probably only ten seconds or so. I wasn't shocked. She had to know. This woman had been studying me like a lab rat for more than twenty years. I was a bit surprised that she had decided to spring it on me here, now.

"No, I answered, I don't feel a thing. And neither do you apparently. I've always kind of wondered, does that make me a bad person?"

"It certainly could," she replied, "but it definitely doesn't have to, and that is why we're here today. I know you—probably better than anyone else on the planet. You, sir, are a sociopath, just like me. But also like me, you have been gifted with the mixed blessing of knowing what is right and wrong. We may not be able to feel it, but we know it. And unlike normal people, we can act on it, and that's what makes you and me so valuable. We can do things others can't—we can right wrongs no one else can. We can help the world in ways that other people can only dream of. . . ."

She trailed off a bit at this point, almost acknowledging that she had laid a whole lot of shit on me in a very short time. Less time than it takes to eat a single burrito.

"No offense AJ," which is what I have been calling her for as long as I can remember, "but who the hell are you? I've never heard you talk like this before, and that's an awful big pile of shit you just dumped here. What exactly do you do? What do you want me for? And more importantly, is any of it worth it?"

She laughed out loud as she listened, as if she could have predicted every question I would ask, every word I would say.

"Absolutely yes, it's worth it. And I am in a position to make a lot of things happen, and I could use your help. But if you decide to join me, there is probably no turning back. So don't take it lightly. But this I promise you, there's a lot in this world that 'bad' people like us can do that can bring about good things. But it requires commitment. One you can't possibly make now, but maybe soon."

It suddenly occurred to me about my dad and how this could have something to do with him.

"Does my dad know about you—about this?" I asked.

"Yes," she answered, "but try to discuss it with him as little as possible. Both for your protection and your parents'. That was part of the deal I made with them. Please respect that."

"He isn't like us, is he?" I asked, already knowing the answer. "He felt every bit of what he had to do?"

"Yes," Jane answered. "And he knows we will do the right

things, but don't ever slap him in the face with it. He wasn't built for that. And I am glad he wasn't."

This was definitely not a conversation I was expecting. Aunt Jane was a wonderful aunt and just a bit of a mystery woman. Remember when I said that she was constantly asking about my feelings. But she almost never shared anything about herself. Her main home was in Reston, Virginia, for as long as I could remember. Before today her description of her work was of a mind-numbingly dull job in the federal bureaucracy. But even as a kid it never quite seemed to add up. She possessed a certain confidence that was inconsistent with that of a pencil pusher.

A while back I had asked my father about her and he'd told me, "She works for the Federal Government in some way— who knows what?" I was about to find out what that was. Well, some of it anyway. Even then I knew that she would always remain a mystery.

She explained that she was in position to recruit, train, and handle what she called "operatives" in various parts of the U.S. government. It was something of a specialty. She had seen something in me. Raw and undeveloped, but still something.

We were close. She knew that, while formally uneducated, I was intelligent, curious, and spongelike in my retention. She knew that I had spent a lifetime learning the physical tools of a sniper. Not the full preparation, but my dad had done the setting up—that skill of shooting something from a long distance.

So I took the initiative.

"So, what exactly do you want from me?" I asked.

"To be honest," she said, "all of you. If you take my offer your life will change forever. Your identity will be all but erased, you will have no permanent home, and you will be in near constant danger. You may be able to retire someday, but don't count on it." Her eyes locked on mine as she spoke. "That is most, but certainly not all, of the bad news. You may, but very likely will not, have a family of your own. But it's not impossible."

At this point I laughed just a little. Was there anything good about this bizarre, sprawling proposal? I was assuming there had to be some upside because, despite the obvious, I am not a complete idiot. And it's true, I am most definitely a sociopath, but I still kind of hoped to have something of a normal life.

Again, it seemed as if she could read my mind. "You will not have anything that resembles a normal life. It may very well be a fruitful and enjoyable life, maybe even satisfying in a way. You will make a positive effect on the world, even if it doesn't always seem that way in the moment. And you will always have enough money. But normal? Not a fucking chance. But let's be honest, that would probably be true whether you sign up or not. And my guess is that you already know that."

"So, for the sake of argument," I said, "what would happen now?"

"You would leave soon," she replied. "You would be provided with a new identity, maybe several. But at first, at least, your name will be John Frum. When we begin, I will create an entirely new person, including birth records, passports, and a lot of things you don't even need to know about. You would spend the next year or so learning the things you need to know besides shooting a sniper rifle. You will need to learn a lot about small arms, not quite military expert level but pretty close. You will have to learn some basics of hand-to-hand combat, but if you ever need to use it, that means somebody, probably you, fucked up. And when you are ready, you will do what we both know you were always born to do. Kill shitty people."

Again, she had kept my gaze every moment that she spoke. I have no idea what she expected to see. My face never changed. If it was surprise she expected, she most certainly would have been disappointed. But I think she herself might have been surprised with my next question.

"I understand that this can't be a safe line of work for me, but what about my mom and dad. Would they be endangered in any way?"

For the first time, Jane seemed something less than supremely confident. Finally, she answered. "Look, can I guarantee their safety? No. I can't guarantee anyone's safety. But they are my family too. And as you know, I can no more 'feel' that bond than you can. But you have my word that I will protect them to the best of my ability. And if that's not good enough, then I completely understand if you walk away, and I will think no less of you for it."

A few minutes went by where we didn't speak. We were sitting in a sparsely filled Chipotle dining room on those industrial steel stools that made even my very young and strong back ache. I think we were just content to absorb the fast, but impactful conversation of moments before.

Jane spoke as if she had been thinking about what to say for a few minutes. "I thought about lying to your parents about the nature of your employment. But with their background, there was just no way it was going to fly. What could I tell them? We need you to be a taxidermist? It would have been pointless."

Over my shoulder I began to hear the conversation at a nearby table. I shouldn't have been able to—I have no special hearing ability—but the couple in their late thirties seated nearby grew louder and louder.

"I told you no fucken tomatoes!" the man shouted in a tone and volume normally reserved for a Cocker Spaniel that has pissed on your couch. "If you don't like it, then order it yourself next time, you ludicrous douchebag," the woman answered.

I had to give her some credit for the creative use of insults. But it was still obnoxious. There weren't many people in the dining room, but the occupants of the six or so tables turned to look at the delightful couple. Except Jane and myself. We continued to eat, occasionally glancing at each other.

Aunt Jane broke the silence. "Do you suppose the world would suffer any great loss if those two were no longer with us?" she asked, looking up to gauge my reaction. As she said that, an extremely loud car went by, delaying my response.

The dining room we were sitting in was a good thirty-five feet from the adjacent road and separated by glass windows and a closed door. Yet the sound from that car was so loud that everyone in the dining room stopped what they were doing. Several people winced in discomfort.

"And what about that asshole? Everywhere he goes in that thing makes the world an ever so slightly worse place. Do you figure the rest of us could learn to get along without him?"

My sense of justice kicked in and I said, "C'mon, AJ, is it really that big a deal? They're just everydayassholes—they're everywhere. Honestly, do they deserve to die just for being a pain in the ass?"

"Honestly?" Jane replied. "When someone says 'honestly,' does that mean they're being honest?"

"Who gives a shit," I answered. "It's sort of beside the point. I asked you if these assholes deserved to die just because they are annoying?"

"Honestly," she replied sarcastically, "I'm not sure, and you know what else, neither are you. Because, for the record, when someone says 'honestly,' what follows is usually actually honest. Yes—honest—but uncertain. Almost as if the person saying it is trying to convince themselves as much as they are you. But you want an answer, and the answer is yes—they probably have it coming. Are you shocked?"

It took me a moment with my wheels spinning before finally asking, "Is this my job? Are you saying you want me to go around killing annoying people?"

"No, not as such," she answered. "But to be honest," she

continued, her face conveying the irony of her use of that word, "I don't really mind. If you want to, and it doesn't interfere with your work, then go ahead and dispense justice as you see fit. I trust your instincts because I know them. They are the same as mine. I mean, let's face it, a homicidal sociopath can kill anyone without remorse. It may not be perfect, but killing assholes is certainly better than going around killing random botanists or *Star Wars* fans. Although some of them are pretty annoying. But don't get caught and don't let it interfere with my assignments for you—ever." She let that hang in the air long enough, and to the point where I didn't have to ask what it might mean for me to violate that simple set of rules.

"So, Mr. Frum," she said, using my new name for the first time. "Did you happen to notice the woman in a pink T-shirt enter the restaurant? How about the man behind you whose gait suggests he's wearing a weapon in an ankle holster—did you notice him?"

This wasn't a fair question in that she was seated in a corner of the restaurant facing the front door and could see all the patrons, anyone who entered, and every staff member in the front of the house. I was seated opposite her and could observe none of that without turning around.

"No," I finally answered, despite it having been a foregone conclusion. "Why is he wearing an ankle holster, John? Is he a criminal, a cop, a civilian? What do you think?" I thought for a moment without turning around.

"I don't know," I admitted. "It's not a fair question, AJ. You can see him. I can't."

"You're right, John, it's not a fair question. Even less fair because there is no gun, there is not even a man. I made it up. Before you ask why, I want you to consider the first lesson in your new career. Watch everything. You never know what's important and, as time goes by, you will learn to know what is important and what just is. And by important, I mean things that can hurt you. Any public place you go, you must learn to watch everything, everyone. After a while, it becomes second nature. So much so that you will always be seated where I am instead of where you are."

"Thank you" seemed to be the only appropriate response, but there were still plenty of unanswered questions if I was to go along with this. Although, if I am being honest with myself —something most sociopaths are particularly good at—I already knew I was going to do it.

"So now what?" I asked. "What do I do now?"

"Well, John, there's not much for you to do at the moment. I will need a month or so to get everything ready, and when I do you will leave here and probably not be back for quite a while, if ever. So say your goodbyes. As a military brat, that's something you're used to doing. Tell people you are leaving for school, which wouldn't be too far from the truth. Which actually leads me to lesson number two. Never lie when the truth will do. In fact, try not to lie at all. Save your lies for matters of self-preservation. It's easier, less taxing on your memory, and it makes a person happier."

I interrupted her at that point and asked, "Happier? I think I am the happiest person I know, except for maybe you?"

"I know, John, that is part of how I knew that you were right for the job. Just sit tight for a month or so and we will get this going."

I would have more questions for her later, but for now all I could muster was, "Hey, thanks for the burrito, AJ. It was pretty good."

FOUR

That went pretty well. I have been studying this child since days after his birth, so there weren't a lot of surprises. I was pleased when he pushed back on the concept of killing. It meant he had at least some sense of justice and wouldn't just run around killing people at random. Like most people his age, he was oblivious to the world around him. He's going to need to fix that. But he will have help. A lot of help.

He doesn't know it yet, but he is going to New Mexico. To a house on a large tract of land that technically speaking is part of the National Park Service. Though you won't find Yogi Bear or friendly park rangers wandering around. It's a training facility. It has an indoor shooting range, an outdoor shooting range, a classroom, a boxing gym, a gymnastics room, and a weight room. John will be using most of it and he will be there for about a year, depending on his progress. His trainers will be brought in, usually one at a time. He will also be assigned a psychologist dedicated specifically to working with him.

He won't be a prisoner there, but the closest town is nearly a forty-five-minute drive. Most of what he needs will be brought in, but he will have a car and can drive into town whenever he wants, if it doesn't interfere with training. For the time being, he is on the payroll of the National Park Service and might remain so even after his "graduation."

My only regret is that I am taking him in so young. No matter how much we train him, it's still too early. The ideal recruitment age for this type of work is about thirty. He's too young. But he's also my nephew and I know him as well as anyone besides myself. And the only reason I know myself better is because I have made it my business to do so.

The average lifespan of someone in this type of service is just over seven years. So it can be said that I have sentenced my nephew to a death before thirty-five. And that may be true. But I, too, am a sociopath and, therefore, feel no guilt. It's simply a calculation. I believe he can do so much good that it's worth it. Also, an average is just an average. There is no guarantee that he will not live to a ripe old age. The odds are against it, sure, but by no means certain. And this is a particularly suitable and talented boy. I believe that he can beat those odds. And since I am a sociopath, you can believe that my thoughts on the matter are not tilted by the fact that he is my "beloved" nephew.

"John," like me, is happy. And that fact alone should be enough to make you realize that there is something wrong with us mentally. The base mindset of almost all of humanity is anxiety. I can't help but laugh when I read articles that tell us that chronic anxiety is a symptom of modern man or a sick society or culture. Bullshit! Anxiety is built into us at the molecular level. Our ancient ancestors, the very people whose blood courses through our veins, lived in a constant state of fear and anxiety. That is a large part of why they survived long enough to pass on those genes to us. I assure you that all of their relaxed neighbors became the breakfast of a passing predator.

Relaxation and calm were a luxury that they definitely could not afford. We are born to be nervous, anxious, and to a great extent greedy and unhappy. We are biologically programmed to always want more. To never be satisfied with what we have. We are machines programmed to eat, fuck, and gather as many things as possible to make sure we can continue to eat and fuck. Happiness and satisfaction are most definitely and completely abnormal. We are biologically programmed to run around the planet with the only goal being to survive so we can continue running around the planet. And to pass these genes on to others so that they can run around the planet for a while too. But what I find most interesting about our current culture is an obsession by many, if not most people, to seek attention for its own sake. We live in a world of constant input. It is almost impossible to escape. Media, social media, advertising, traffic, billboards, and a million other things compete for our attention. With social media, we at least have the opportunity to answer the onslaught with our own posts and content. Never have we had such a microphone, yet never have we had less to say. But perversely, instead of giving the common person a voice, social media has just served to drown us in input even further. Our collective response has been an almost pathological desire to be seen and heard by somebody—anybody! The result has been obnoxious, to say the least. We all speak louder, play our music louder. We drive our cars faster and more aggressively. We say nonsensical things to strangers on the internet. Words we would never utter to a person standing in front of us. It's as if our national id has been unleashed and is wreaking havoc on our society, not unlike Godzilla laying waste to 1960s Tokyo.

This isn't just my opinion. On my computer desktop are hundreds of studies that conclude that we as a culture have become the equivalent of the homeless man on the subway screaming and pulling his pants down. I study much of it professionally due to the actual national security threats some of it presents from both groups and individuals. But as a person and something of a scientist, I am grotesquely fascinated by it because it is truly an evolutionary anomaly. Attention seeking in the abstract would be part of our need for good standing in our community to help assure our survival. Gaining attention for being the one who brought the animal carcass to our primitive tribal members would garner positive attention. Evolution clearly favored such behavior. But posting a stupid, incorrect, and nonsensical meme on Facebook would offer no such advantage. Attention seeking for its own sake is in no way a biological imperative. In fact, being quiet and avoiding the attention of predators is the biological imperative. It's also really fucken annoying in countless ways. And it can get you in trouble.

Some of this behavior rises to the level of commanding my attention. Which I can assure you has turned out quite poorly for the attention seekers. I suppose the same negatives apply in everyday life. Also with negative, but less fatal results.

We are born into a world of constant danger. So much so that we must push ninety-nine percent of those dangers out of our minds just to function on a day-to-day basis. Disease, war, famine, drought, tornadoes, and even gout for Christ's sake. There are so many things that can kill, harm, and maim our fragile and delicate bodies. And what's more, we are "blessed" with the cognitive ability to know our own fragility and mortality. As much as technology has changed things only serves as a reminder that we can vanish from existence at any moment. If we get sick or unlucky, we can be homeless and hungry, struggling for the very basics of survival. And we know all of this every minute of every day.

But it gets even worse. These little meat puppets we inhabit require constant maintenance and begin decaying almost the moment they are minted. If you are not miserable or anxious, you are almost definitely high or crazy. And this is for the lucky ones among us. Now imagine wandering the globe while black or female or gay or, as sometimes happens, literally attached to another meat puppet. In general, I am a rather harsh critic of human behavior and I have tools at my disposal that can create dire consequences for those who run afoul of my judgment. Yet, I am quite forgiving when it comes to the things people do that might make them feel just a little bit better, providing it creates no harm to others. Because life, to put it simply, is hard.

Everything can and does go wrong. Virtually all the time. For everyone. And our modern world is designed to exploit our entirely natural and warranted fear and anxiety. Religious hucksters, drug dealers, and salesmen stand at the ready to exploit our fears and fragility. Taking our money, time, and in the case of the Catholic Church, our children.

So what am I doing here? Why am I doing it? As a sociopath I feel no empathy or pity for the human condition. I don't weep for the sorry state of natural existence. But I would still like to believe that we are more than the sum of our fears.

We are a child species with giant brains and opposable thumbs as our only real tools of survival. And we have become more than capable of causing our own demise. Modern humans in the current world are little more than teenagers with a bottle of whiskey and the car keys. It's just a matter of time.

And that's where I come in. The authorization for the work I do was born in the aftermath of World War II and the dawn of the Cold War. It was President Eisenhower who saw and understood the danger of our situation firsthand. I think he may have been the first to truly understand the existential threat that we had become to ourselves. He had the power and the wherewithal to create us. I won't bore you with the details of our funding and organization. But Eisenhower saw to it that we would outlive him, and we did.

I am the seventh person to serve in this role and the second woman. I could give you a list of those who served before me, but you would probably recognize one, or perhaps two names. Neither of whom would be known for what we actually do. Which is to protect this country from itself and others. And in a larger sense to protect the world from the United States. Because regardless of what you have probably been taught, the greatest threat to the world would be a rogue United States. It's quite simple really. The United States is a far greater threat to itself and others than any foreign foe is to the United States. Don't get me wrong. Eisenhower was truly the ultimate patriot and he assured that our first loyalty will always be to this country. But he also understood that, with the tools at our disposal, we would have to be nearly perfect in order for the world to avoid total annihilation. And no country, not even one as great as this one, approaches perfection. And there may be times that the world would need protection *from* us rather than *by* us.

So we fight the threats from within and without with the tools we have been given. And I believe "John" will be an exceptionally useful tool.

He will be trained in a way that only a handful of people in human history have ever been trained. Not that he will be an elite "super spy" in the conventional sense. But he will be given a select set of abilities that will enable him to survive, live, and fulfill his purpose. For instance, we will try to get him fluent in Spanish, Russian, and Mandarin, but he will not be force fed. If he has the ability he will be taught. He will learn basic computer skills, including cybersecurity and how to get around it, but he will still be far from an elite hacker. He will be taught how to create quick and memorable psychological profiles of people he meets and to gather useful information. He will be introduced to a very wide but shallow pool of skills. He will be the jack of many trades but the master of only one. And that is the skill he already possesses—to be a remote and remorseless assassin. He will erase his victims from a mile away, literally. And in some circumstances even further. If this boy ever needs to fight with his fists, he will be ready. But that will mean that he, us, or both have fucked up somehow. The school bell is about to ring, and he will be right on time for class.

FIVE

My father was waiting for me when I got home from lunch with Aunt Jane. It was immediately obvious that he wanted to speak with me. My mother was out shopping for groceries, and he was in the living room. The television was on but with the volume turned down. He sat upright in a recliner chair and motioned for me to sit.

"So how was lunch with Aunt Jane?" he asked.

Given what my aunt had told me, I was a little surprised at his directness. My hesitance reflected my uncertainty about how to respond. So I settled on the mundane, for the moment.

"We went to Chipotle. It's always pretty good," I replied innocently.

"You know damn well that's not what I'm talking about, so tell me, what you are going to do, even though I can bet that I already know the answer."

"I'm going to do it, Dad, if for no other reason than the training. No matter what, learning this stuff will be good and maybe lead to a career outside her world."

He hesitated a moment as if he was measuring his words carefully. "Bullshit yourself if you need to, but don't bullshit me.

I'm sure she already told you that this is almost certainly a one-way ticket. I'm not telling you not to do it. But be honest with yourself. You want to do it. And I don't blame you. What young man, even one as rational and unusual as you, could resist what she has to offer? Just so you know, she made me the same offer years ago. But I think she knew I would turn it down. She knows I'm not like you—or her."

I was a bit surprised by his confession.

"Dad, we both know I'm different, that she's different. It's not something to be proud of, but it's true and always will be."

"So do it, son, but make no mistake. Your Aunt Jane loves you, and me and your mom for that matter. At least as much as she is capable of. But she will never hesitate to do what she needs to do that will protect her mission and the overall good. And if you become a liability to that goal, she will do whatever is necessary." He stared straight into my eyes as he spoke. There was no mistaking the meaning. If I became a liability, she would eliminate me. She wouldn't be happy about it, but she would do it all the same. "You will have the chance to do great things. You have the rare opportunity to change the world for the better. But please, please, do not cross your aunt."

The point could not have been clearer. And, of course, I would never cross her, but I still knew so little about what my assignments would be or even exactly what it might mean to cross her. My dad added, "I'm actually going to be the one to start your training. She wants you to start working with moving targets while you're waiting for her to be ready for you. We have at least a month. And I will rig up targets that simulate the movement of a person. It's a whole different thing hitting a moving target, and even more so when it's a living moving target."

I asked him, "Why is a live target so much different than any other moving target?"

"The most primal reason of all. They want to live."

"They'll never see it coming, Dad. You know that."

His dad was silent for a moment, measuring his words carefully. "I shot and killed sixty-five people during my tours in Iraq and Afghanistan. I also missed five times." Now, this was shocking. In my mind, at least, it seemed impossible that he could ever miss, I don't care how much the target was moving. If he had a clear line of sight, he would hit it. "I know what you're thinking—how could I have missed? Well, a couple of them were in stationary vehicles and the glare threw me off. But there were at least two misses where I had no excuse at all. I just missed. And to this day I wonder how many other people died because I failed to take out those targets."

This was by far the most emotional I had ever seen him and the deepest conversation we'd ever had. That alone was enough to make me understand the gravity of the choice I was making. "I will make you and Mom proud, Dad, and Aunt Jane too."

"I know you will, son. What do say we go do a little shooting? We might as well get started."

The next month went by slowly. Especially since it ended up being closer to seven weeks until I got word from Jane that everything was in place for my training.

Jane called me on my regular cell phone. It was the first time we had spoken since that day in Chipotle. She said this would be the last time we would communicate on any conventional devices. When I asked what that meant, she replied that I would know soon enough. She told me to expect a package in a few days with instructions, a plane ticket, and some other documents. I needed only to follow the instructions. The rest of my questions would be answered when I reached my destination, wherever the hell that would be.

As usual, she was true to her word. The package was delivered three days later. Inside was a passport, complete with my picture. How she got that picture I still don't know, but it was a proper passport photo. There was also a New Mexico driver's license, again complete with my picture. Finally, there were airline tickets to Santa Fe, New Mexico. All of the documents were in the name of this brand-new person, John Frum. Ever since she had first said that name back at the restaurant, it had felt somewhat familiar. And since it was now going to be my name, I googled it.

John Frum was a god. During World War II, U.S. and British naval vessels visited at least fifty south Pacific islands that had never been visited or touched by the outside world. We tend to think of them as being all the same and paint them all with the same brush. Weird, exotic islands with cannibals and savages. But the truth is they are as different from each other as they are from us. They are, for the most part, quite distant and separate from each other, and each had developed their own unique cultures. But they shared one thing in common. None of them had ever seen anything like us before. Mostly pale white men in starched white uniforms who traveled in massive ships bristling with weapons. These men brought food and radios and medicines and all they asked in return was safe harbor. On at least twenty of these islands, the men from the ships became legends. And in time the legends became religions. There were variations in the legends, but the consistent theme was of a benevolent god, traveling by ship and bestowing wealth and good fortune on the islands by way of cargo. Historians refer to these collective ideologies as cargo cults. The most common of the cargo cults are known as John Frum cults. Nobody is sure how that came about. The best theory is that, to the islanders, "John from America" became "John Frum" the god. Most of the religions involved the eventual return of John Frum bringing the motherlode of cargo. Spreading wealth, health, and redemption for those who believed.

There are still close to four million people who practice some form of a John Frum religion, despite the fact that these islands, eighty years later, are quite aware of the outside world and the perfectly mortal people of Great Britain and America. Before you laugh, consider the logic of their religion and compare it to whatever flavor of spirituality you practice. And then consider that there are people still alive who have actually seen their god.

Not surprisingly, it was very clever of Jane to use that as a cover name for my identity. Anyone who googled John Frum would be swamped with thousands of pages of cargo cult lore before they would stumble on any information about any actual person.

The flight to Santa Fe was only two days later, but I was more than ready. I was told only to pack toiletries and as much clothing as I could fit in a carry-on. I was not to check a bag. I was not to bring my cell phone or any other electronics. Apparently, I would be doing some shopping in New Mexico. There would be someone at the airport to pick me up that Jane said "I would not miss." I immediately pictured a man running up and down the concourse yelling, "Frum! Frum! Spy guy Frum!"

My father drove me to the airport. I'd said goodbye to my mother back at home. There were no tears, but my mother hugged me tightly. More than ever before. It was nice. And I thought there was a chance that I might miss her. That I might miss them both. In that moment, I truly felt that I was her little boy. Or more like I sensed *her* feeling that.

The ride was uneventful and the conversation technical. Both of us avoiding the subject that it might be quite some time before we saw each other again. It was not an absolute that I could never come home. I had been told not to expect it, but it was not out of the question. Jane was also going to provide a secure cell phone for my parents. I could call that number, but they couldn't call me. So, I could be in contact with them, but Jane had made it clear that there could be long stretches of time that I would not be available to them for one reason or another.

He dropped me off at the curb. There was no long goodbye.

"I love you, son. You are going to be the best . . . but don't let it go to your head," he said with a soft chuckle.

"I love you too, Dad. I will make you and Mom proud."

"I know you will—but it's more important to make your aunt proud. That's how you'll stay alive."

I nodded, grabbed my small bag, and stepped onto the curb and into a new life.

SIX

The flight was uneventful, and a few hours later I walked out of the Santa Fe Airport. Jane was right, my ride was pretty easy to find. Just to the left of the door I came out of was a man leaning against a nondescript black SUV holding a large white sign with FRUM spelled out with a dark green Sharpie. I think he recognized me. I walked up to him and said "I'm your guy."

"Welcome to New Mexico," he replied while opening the back door and grabbing my bag.

Once we were both inside, he started out of the airport and told me that it was over an hour drive, and I should make myself comfortable. I asked him where we were going. He replied that his instructions were to keep conversation to a minimum.

"No offense intended, sir."

"None taken," I replied. "I understand."

So we spent the rest of the drive in silence as the path went from interstate highway to regular highway to narrow one-lane roads and then finally to dirt roads. I had always wondered about the "middle of nowhere." I mean, if you are nowhere, how do you know where the "middle" is? We were more and more nowhere with every minute as he drove down a series of dirt or gravel roads. The terrain was typical New Mexico. Mostly desert with sparse growth, rocks, and an almost sandy orange feel to everything except the cacti. Which were everywhere.

Finally, I could see a big southwestern-style home at the end of a long dirt driveway. There was a single vehicle adjacent to the house. It was another nondescript black SUV with a New Mexico plate. I hadn't taken notice of the plate of the car I rode in. It doesn't matter, but noticing those kinds of details is exactly what Jane was trying to tell me with her whole "guy with an ankle holster" thing back at Chipotle.

We pulled up in front. I grabbed my bag, hopped out, and said thank you to the driver, who immediately circled and pulled off.

So here was my home for the next year or so. I walked up to the front door, which was unlocked, so I just let myself in, wondering if there was anyone here. The car in the driveway offered no clue. It could just as easily be my car, which as it turns out, it was. I found myself in a pretty ordinary living room. Brown carpet, a couple of beige fabric couches, a couple of rugs, and a stairway to my left. Presumably the bedrooms were upstairs as there was no sign of any on the first floor. I can live with this, I thought, as I walked into the kitchen and found it to be in the same style. Sort of a late nineties southwestern decor of assorted browns and beiges. But with a newer looking light brown hardwood floor that continued throughout the entire downstairs except the living room. Also there was Aunt Jane, quietly seated at the kitchen table.

"How was the flight, John?" She asked, as if this was a normal event, which I guess for her it was.

"Not bad," I answered, matching her nonchalance.

"When did they stop giving away peanuts on airplanes? I was kind of looking forward to them."

"Well, like most things, John, there is a short answer and a long one, but it's mostly because humans are stuffed full of antibiotics and microplastics and are becoming allergic to everything, especially peanuts for some reason."

"Was that the short answer or the long answer?" I joked in response, but she made it clear that it was time to get to business.

"John, there is a very good chance that you and I won't see each other ever again. We will speak a lot, but we won't see each other for a long time, or perhaps ever. And at the risk of being sentimental, I wanted to see my favorite nephew." That was probably true, but the real reason was just as likely to be the briefing I was just about to get.

She motioned toward a box full of documents and devices on the kitchen counter. I brought the box over to the table and sat down next to her. There were five identical cell phones and two large tablets. There were also passports, driver's licenses, credit cards, debit cards, and birth certificates. Apparently, I had been born in Nebraska to the no-doubt-very-proud Frum family. There was one set of documents in the name of *John Brian Louis*. She saw the look of puzzlement on my face and said, "Those are your 'go' documents. If shit ever hits the fan, those are the docs you will use to leave the country and disappear if that should ever become necessary. But one important thing. You will still need the Frum identity to access your personal finances."

"Money? I have money?" I asked half kidding.

"Yes, John, this is a job after all. A weird one, yes, but still a job. Here's how it works. You make five thousand a week, tax free. The money will be wired to an account in the Cayman Islands quarterly. You will gain access to that account after your training is complete, but the pay starts today." She paused long enough to gauge my reaction before continuing, "Yes, that's about 260K a year. The trick is to live long enough to spend it. I'm hoping for ten good years out of you, so with interest you can expect to have about three million dollars lying around. More or less enough to retire on if you choose to—and if you live long enough. If something happens to you, whatever money is in there will go to your folks. And not that you asked, but while you're working you will have no expenses of your own. You will pay for everything with those debit cards from a single bank account. You will have access to the account from your phones, all of which are identical and have the same number. By the way, you and I will speak on those phones and only those phones. Our conversations are a hundred percent secure. You may also use them for other calls, but if you are talking to anyone other than me, then you must assume the line is not secure. Not even with your parents. In other words, don't be a putz. I need you to treat every conversation with anyone but me as if someone is listening. You are going to learn a lot over the next year, but what I just told you might be the single most important lesson. Treat every phone like it is a hot microphone—because it just might be."

That was a lot for me to digest in a short period of time and, honestly, I was a little tired from the trip. She seemed to sense it.

"Look, John, you will have a lot of questions as we go along. You don't have to absorb everything today. Rest today and tomorrow. On Wednesday, you will get a visit from a counselor."

"You mean a shrink?"

"Yes, a psychiatrist. And if it was anyone other than you, I would say yes, she's a shrink. But in your case, since I know you so well, she really is more like your counselor. You will find this to be a lonely business, John. And everyone, even sociopaths, need someone to talk to that they can be really honest with.

And in your line of work there is only one person you can be honest with—me. And even I can't really fill that role for you because I'm your boss. And it keeps me from being the truly impartial advocate that everyone needs. So, unless you absolutely hate her, she will probably come see you every couple of weeks, and she will be on call for you all the time, even once you are in the field. But remember, calls to her cannot be considered secure either, so if you really need her, then ask her to come to you. She will. We will start sending trainers in a few days, and I will text you a schedule of your training each week. When you aren't training, your time is your own. You can come and go as you please. The car outside is for you. But the nearest real town is about forty minutes away. I expect you to cook and clean for yourself and you will find a pretty well-equipped little gym upstairs. I don't need or want you to be ripped. I need you to look ordinary, so don't get all jacked up like an inmate. But stay in shape."

I could read between those lines—don't get fat but don't become Arnold Schwarzenegger either. And I wasn't worried about caring for myself. As an only child, both my mom and dad had passed along some kitchen wisdom. I'm no chef, but I could cook enough to keep me off a steady diet of takeout and fast food. Not to mention that a McDonald's run was an almost two-hour road trip.

Her phone shook and buzzed slightly.

"There's my ride. I want to show you one thing before I go."

She led me over to a door off the kitchen, which in any other house would lead to a garage. We walked through into what was a fully equipped three-lane shooting range. On one side was a wall fixture with no fewer than fifteen different rifles. Most were familiar to me, but there were a few that I had never seen or handled. At least half of them were military quality. Two at least were beyond military grade. Really first-rate, cutting-edge stuff. On the other side were the handguns, probably close to fifty of them. I am by no means a small arms expert, but I could tell that this again was top of the line hardware. There was at least a hundred thousand dollars' worth of weapons in this room.

"OK, John, take the next couple of days to look around and get comfortable. Call me anytime you need me, but always on one of these phones."

I walked with her to the front door where she stopped me.

"Let's say goodbye here. I don't need you to be seen by the driver, so stay inside until we're gone. Good luck, nephew. I love you," she said with a wry smile.

"I love you too," I replied.

Both of us knowing what that meant—we felt no love. We aren't capable. But in a way, I think that means even more.

SEVEN

It was dark by the time Jane had left, so I figured it was a good time to just get familiar with the house. Upstairs I found two decent-sized bedrooms and a pretty nice, up-to-date bathroom, shower, and tub. There was also the gym she had promised. Downstairs was what I had already seen. A comfortable living room, a kitchen, a shooting range, and an armory with enough firepower to launch a military assault on the Vatican. There was one nice touch from my "sweet" aunt. There was a modern video game console attached to the TV in the living room. Something she knew I enjoyed. I reminded myself to thank her for that. I meant to make myself something to eat in the fully stocked kitchen but never quite got around to it and fell asleep on the couch.

When I woke, I started looking around the grounds. It was a massive piece of property. If I had to guess, I would say twenty acres or more. All of it was surrounded by a five-foot-tall black chain link fence in more or less of a large square. The outdoor shooting range was a three-minute walk from the house. The grounds were also typical New Mexico scrub brush cactus and sand with a lonely looking tree here and there.

I went back to the house with the idea of making some lunch. But instead, I decided to take a drive in the general direction of the nearest town. I didn't take the shortest route, so after about seventy-five minutes I found myself amid the three or four city blocks known as Bluebush. Probably named for the peculiar kind of cactus that sprouted a small blue and homely looking flower of sorts. The town consisted of a few storefronts, offices, restaurants, and a handful of fast-food joints. I guess they were mostly regional places, being that the only ones I recognized were Hardee's and Wendy's. I had lunch at a place called Tex Mex Lex. Combine a regular Applebee's with a shit-kicker redneck bar and you would have a pretty good idea of the place. It was the first time I had to answer a question that I found out later was of supreme importance: green or red?

Chili, or chile depending on who you ask, is serious business in New Mexico. It's a dish, a side dish, a stew, and a sauce that apparently pairs perfectly with everything except breakfast cereal. Being new around here I ordered both, so as not to inadvertently offend anyone. My waitress, a guardedly friendly and weathered late-middle-aged woman was interested in which I thought was better. She stopped by more than once to ask. For the record, I slightly preferred the spice and tang of the red over the meaty flavor of the green. But both were good. I read the room, however, and dutifully reported that green was superior. An answer that seemed to please my host.

I drove directly home from the restaurant so that I would know exactly how far this nearest blot of civilization was. It was exactly forty-two minutes from the restaurant to my front door. I wouldn't be running out for a cup of coffee anytime soon. Bluebush had everything I would need for the next year or so. There was a proper supermarket and a couple other grocery stores. Most of what I need was there, a mere forty-two minutes away. Clothing was almost ninety minutes away, so I would go and get the few things I needed in as few trips as possible. Jane had made it clear that I was not to have anything delivered to the house. I never tried, but it was unlikely anyone would deliver there anyway.

My training began with my therapist's arrival the next afternoon. She was a woman in her early thirties, smartly dressed, carrying a small satchel, and she introduced herself as Kate. I had been expecting her and welcomed her into my new home. Off the kitchen was a small patio area with a table and seating for four. We sat across from each other as we spoke. I had seen an Army therapist a couple of times throughout my youth, and I was not intimidated. I have always thought that pretty much everyone can benefit from their services. It is good to have someone to speak to who has no stake in our lives. We may have well-meaning friends and family to confide in, but all of those people have some bias, some agenda or notion about you that prevents them from being truly objective. A qualified therapist can be invaluable in helping a person around their own bullshit and call them out on it when necessary. But Kate was not quite the uninterested party that a conventional therapist normally is. She works for Jane and her interests, not mine. Her job is to help me to do my job, not necessarily to help *me*. But even knowing this didn't bother me. Nothing was being hidden, and if it's part of my job and my training to talk to her, then I will talk to her. I think she found my attitude to be a little surprising, as if she had expected some resistance. But I was happy to answer her questions and follow where she might lead.

It started with the basics. My age, education, sexuality, and how I felt about my parents. About a half hour in, she asked me an interesting question. "John, have you ever done anything wrong, anything you feel guilty about?"

"Well, that's really two completely different questions," I answered.

"Have I ever felt guilty about anything? No. You know better than that. I can't feel guilty. Have I ever done anything wrong? Well, nobody is perfect. I'm sure I've done plenty of things wrong."

She sat back in her chair and pondered my answer for a few moments before continuing. "How would you know if you did something wrong without guilt to remind you of it?" she asked.

"People can tell you that you did something wrong, but that hardly matters. How do *you* know if you've done something wrong?"

And now it was my turn to ponder.

"Damn, that's a good question," I said as I thought to myself, trying my best to give her an honest answer.

"OK," I said. "I think it's a question of playing the consequences. Let's say I'm driving down the highway without a care in the world, I start to think about you—bam!—I whip out my cock and start jerking off, right there in the car. Going eighty miles per hour and just whacking away. Unfortunately, I'm a bit distracted and I don't see Father Murphy and his illegitimate, slightly cute but very cross-eyed daughter and—splat!—the two of them do significant damage to the front end of my truck. I would hold them responsible. But the fact that they lay dead in a bloody heap prevents them from making any meaningful restitution for my loss. Have I done something wrong? Yes, I think so. But wait!" I yell in my best infomercial voice, "There's more! Father Murphy, as it turns out was a rather prolific pedophile. One hundred or more twelve-year-old boys will be able to sit much more comfortably as the result of my very brave masturbation."

She just sat and stared at me for the better part of a minute, trying unsuccessfully to stifle laughter, before reminding me, "You really are a sick fuck."

"I am," I agreed but now completely serious. "Right and wrong is a tricky business, and everything we do has consequences. But yes, of course I have done things wrong, nothing particularly terrible, nothing that would have caused anything worse than hurt feelings, and I can see and understand that I have done so. But no, I have never experienced guilt at any of those times."

Kate was smiling and scribbling away in her notebook. "I can see why Jane chose you," she said. "You really are an ideal candidate. But that doesn't mean there won't be bumps along the way. And things may change after you complete your first mission. I have a pretty good idea of how you are going to take it. But as you yourself pointed out, there are always unintended consequences. It is my job to be there for you, and I will be—anytime you need me."

She gathered her papers and began loading them in her satchel. "I'll see you a week from today, John, and then after that it will probably be more on the phone. But I will still be dropping by from time to time. And Jane asked me to remind you that when we speak on the phone, we must always assume it's not secure."

"I understand," I replied as I walked her to the door.

"Thanks for everything. I'll see you soon."

The days flew by. I had some form of training at least every other day. The computer guys would come. They would bring their own hardware. A couple of desktops and tablets. They were teaching me cybersecurity and what they called "work-around skills." I have a pretty average aptitude for this type of thing. These guys were all business, very little conversation. But I learned. I had three different personal trainers, one of whom specialized in teaching the basics of hand-to-hand combat and self-defense. Those classes were about ninety minutes each and he came every week. The other two would work me out for about an hour at a time. They would send me a schedule every couple of weeks, but in general one of them was there every other day. They focused on strength training and instructed me to do forty-five minutes of any cardio that I chose. They wanted me to do it every day. I didn't quite live up to that, but I would walk or light run most days depending on the weather. I had a treadmill in the house, but I never used it. It was just too boring. I didn't lose any weight during the training. Since about the time I turned twenty, I had topped out at just under six feet tall and I don't remember ever weighing more than 180 pounds. Six months into my training I was about 175. I didn't exactly look muscular, but I definitely looked and felt the fittest I had ever been. Those guys knew what they were doing.

Three or more different teachers came at one time or another to teach me about small arms. I wasn't a complete novice, and I picked up their teachings pretty easily. These guys struck me as being military, but none wore the uniform, and I knew better than to ask. As Aunt Jane would say, I just "dummied up and learned."

Kate continued to come but her sessions turned more instructional than introspective. She was teaching psychological techniques that therapists like her use to help clients open up. Or perhaps reveal more than they intend to. She taught me tricks of memorization, how to remember places, names, and people. I was enthusiastic and absorbed her teachings easily and thoroughly.

The language stuff was all online but with live instructors. It's not a talent of mine at all and not a whole lot of it stuck. I had been learning Spanish throughout high school, and with the intensive training I was now getting, I improved quite a bit. But I still have only the vocabulary of a Peruvian toddler. Of all the languages I was exposed to, the only one I really took to was Russian. I'm nowhere close to fluent, but it seems to be sticking.

The most work was done at the outdoor shooting range. We spent hundreds of hours on the range. I learned how to use more than ten new weapons. Dozens of new targets were arranged, mostly moving in all different ways, speeds, and conditions. The last few months, almost all of my work was at night. They would even bring lighting to simulate different conditions. Many, many hours were spent outside shooting in wind, rain, and fog. Yes, they brought a machine that produced fog with them. Their job was to make me proficient and on target in every conceivable condition with numerous different weapons. They seemed impressed with my skills, but didn't hesitate to tell me where I might come up short. And each time they came, they left me a to-do list of techniques to work on by myself. And I did. I had committed to this, and I was going to be the best I could be.

About eight months into my training, Kate gave me an assignment. Jane wanted me to learn some basic surveillance skills and, according to Kate, there was no better way to learn than by doing it. I was instructed to choose a person and surveil them. Basically follow them around for three days and then file a mock SSR—standard surveillance report. I have no idea if there really is anything as an SSR or they just made that shit up for me. Anyway, I didn't exactly choose the person at random. It was a guy I "knew" from Tex Mex Lex. I had been stopping by there every week or so for a beer or a meal.

His name was Bob. He drove a shitty old pickup truck and his breath smelled like dog food. I know the truck because I happened to see him leave in it. I knew the breath because this moron had practically laid on top of me on more than one occasion at the bar in an attempt to get yet another shot of shitty well tequila. He played pool occasionally. Got way too shitfaced a little more than occasionally. And was very loud and obnoxious way, way more than occasionally.

To be honest, he had given me ample reason to think about the virtues of killing annoying people. He wasn't a tall guy. He was your typical mid-forties fat white guy who was sure that we now had way too many "spicks" in New Mexico. I know this because he was eager to announce this to anyone and everyone, and loudly. And completely without the irony of being in a state called New Mexico. I chose him because it would be easy. I already had a starting point. Also, because I really was, in the back of my mind at least, thinking about popping him. I had thought a lot about my conversation on the matter with Aunt Jane back at Chipotle. An apparently horrible douchebag could have many other virtues that weren't readily apparent when they are literally laying on you and acting like a drunken asshole. This would be a chance to find out and complete my homework at the same time.

I started by following Bob home from the bar late the next night. It was 1 a.m. Friday morning. I was supposed to follow him throughout the weekend. He lived in a pretty well-kept trailer park just a couple of miles from the bar. There was no chance of his "making" me. He wasn't completely shitfaced, but it was a fair bet that if he had been pulled over, he would have blown drunk. I followed him home, and when he got there, I just drove past and kept going as he parked. Then I drove around the block for a couple of minutes after giving him enough time to stumble out of his truck and into the trailer. There was a shitty old Ford sedan in the driveway that he parked behind. I parked across the street and cut my engine. From there I could record the address and make some notes on the home. It wasn't terrible as trailers go. It was clean and fairly new, no junk to the front or side. There was no lawn, so I had no lawncare habits to note. But overall, it was a decent place in decent shape with, like in many trailer parks, the neighbors on both sides being way to close for my taste. I drove around the block again and found an inconspicuous place to park on the other side of the street about two doors down. From there I could easily see when anyone came or went. I had seen lights come on in the home, but there was no sound or conversation, and then the trailer went dark. My friend Bob still had the wherewithal to shut off the lights before passing out. I cheated a little bit. I had a magnetic GPS device that was synced to my phone. I just calmly walked over and quietly put it under his bumper in the back wheel well. This way when I followed him, I could keep my distance without worrying about losing him.

I set the alarm on my phone for 6:30 a.m., roughly five hours later. I figured he wasn't going anywhere for a while. I turned everything off, made sure the doors were locked and put my seatback as far flat as it would go. Not exactly comfortable but good enough. It wasn't long before I fell asleep.

Turns out I timed it pretty well. About a quarter to 7, there was Bob all dressed for work and ready to go. He hopped in his truck and off he went. Of course, I followed at a safe distance. I didn't worry too much about staying close. If I lost him, I could always pick him up again with the GPS. His first stop was Wendy's. For a good all-American breakfast of salt, fat, and sugar, deep fried and poured into a bowl. I don't actually have any idea what he ordered, but it's a pretty safe bet that not a bit of it was healthy. I drove past him as he entered the Wendy's drive-thru. I went down the road a bit and turned around. And once again my timing was good, and he was just pulling back on the road.

It wasn't more than three minutes until he pulled into a trailer and motor home sales lot that I presumed was his workplace. Again, I just drove past and went a couple more miles before turning around. Across the street from Southwest Trailer and Service was a business that sold garden items. Stone statues, some local items you could plant in your yard, and a lot of gravel and stone for driveways and the like. I parked in their lot facing Bob's place and just hung out for a while. There wasn't much to see for quite some time. For those of you who aren't in law enforcement, I'd like to enlighten you to the fact that surveillance work is incredibly boring, except for when it's terrifying. I knew a friend who did insurance work, following around people who were involved mostly in slip-and-fall scam lawsuits. He would find and photograph them chopping wood, playing hockey and doing a bunch of other things that a seriously injured victim could not do. He told me that the handful of times he got "made" did not go well. Guns pulled, threats made.

I didn't think Bob was much of a threat beyond boredom. From what I could tell, he was a salesman. Straight out of central casting. Short-sleeve shirt with a tie that was short to the point where it made it only about halfway down the contours of his huge, well-earned belly. He mostly walked around the large, sandy lot, occasionally stopping to smoke a cigarette or have a short, but I'm sure insightful conversation with a coworker.

I toyed with the idea of wandering onto the lot as a potential customer, but thought better of it, as there was no real upside.

After a while I left and made my way over to *Tex Mex Lex* for some red chili and conversation. I returned to watch the remainder of his excruciatingly long work day. As far as I could see, he spoke with only three potential buyers in almost nine hours. He showed each of them several RVs. But as far as I could tell, all of them left without buying one.

I was actually feeling sorry for the guy and grateful that I had chosen this profession. Avoiding the drudgery of a nine-to-five.

At quitting time, I watched him get in the truck and I followed him, just in case he was going somewhere other than home. He wasn't. He went straight back to the trailer, and I dropped off a mile or so before he got there so as not to get made. I went back to TML and just hung out, checking my GPS app every few minutes for when and if he left home. I didn't have to wait long. Bob popped through the door, still in his work clothes and headed straight to the bar. He loudly announced to the thirty or so customers that it was time to "drink some dinner" and ordered up a double tequila. I will say one thing for the man. When it comes to drinking, he has speed out of the gate. By this point it was about 7:30 and I didn't figure he would be up to anything beyond his normal douchebaggery, so I had some dinner. Actual food. And then hung out for a couple more hours before heading home. I could keep track of him with the GPS and get a little sleep.

Saturday morning, I completed my bio of Bob to report to Jane. Before that I didn't even know his last name. All I had to do was call the trailer place where he worked. I told them I was a customer and Bob had helped me, but I had lost his business card and couldn't remember his last name.

"You talking about Bobby Bush?" the woman on the phone asked me.

"Yes" I said. "White guy, fortyish, kinda heavy set—"

She interrupted me, "Yeah, that's Bobby Bush. He'll be back first thing Monday morning, but if you need anything just swing by and we'll take care of you."

She was friendly and I just told her that I would come back on Monday to see Bob. The rest was just as easy. I just googled "Bob Bush New Mexico," which yielded only three results, one of which was much older and the other much younger than my Bob. Five minutes later I knew he was Robert George Bush. No relation to the presidents, but he was born in Texas a little over forty-seven years ago. I dutifully reported this information to Jane and Kate, who would no doubt do a more thorough check. If for no other reason than to make sure I wasn't just blowing off the assignment and mailing it in. So, I schlepped back to Bluebush to see what our friend was up to this fine Saturday. The answer was shopping. I arrived by his trailer just in time to see him and his wife heading out. Her name was Sheila, as I had learned from my search. They had one daughter together, Shayna, who was twenty-seven years old. Sheila, like Bob, was on the shorter side and carried more than a few extra pounds. I didn't leave when they left the trailer park. Rather I just waited a few minutes and let the GPS tell me where they were off to, which was a town about a half hour away that had a Costco, a Walmart, and a McDonald's. Before their adventure was over, they had visited all three and were back home to the trailer fully fed and stocked up, by 3 p.m.

It was a Saturday, so I wasn't surprised about Bob's next destination. He helped his wife bring in all the spoils of their trip. A few cases of water, big packages of toilet paper and paper towels, and groceries. The groceries consisted of mostly potato chips, baked goods, and Costco packages of raw chicken and ground beef. And then it was off to—you guessed it—Tex Mex Lex. He spent the rest of the day and night there. Drinking as only he can and watching college football. It didn't take a lot of spy skills to know that Bob had an opinion on, well, everything. But particularly on these "barely trained animals" he was watching on TV with enthusiastic intensity. Sports betting isn't legal in New Mexico, but it apparently was as common here as anywhere else. And it was abundantly clear that my friend Bob had wagered a good chunk of his trailer selling earnings on the outcomes of these games.

There was just something he didn't like about these pampered, ungrateful athletes that he saw on TV. And the answer was, of course, that most of the players are black. A truth made even clearer when he referred to them as "tar babies." A racial slight so old that I had to look it up. And, as usual, Bob was completely oblivious to the irony that these "pampered babies" were the only ones in this multibillion-dollar industry that don't make any money. Very few of them end up with a valuable degree and way fewer ever turn pro. Even when they do make it to the pro level, it's almost always a short, tenuous trip. There is a reason that the players refer to the NFL as "Not For Long." The average career of an NFL player is less than three years. All of this was lost on my friend Bob. To him it was just a bunch of niggers on TV. That was a word I had never used in my life. But Bob said it about as often as he said double quarter pounder with cheese, which was quite often.

There are times when I think I understand racism. I have to admit that in the military world that I grew up in, racism wasn't much of a thing. At least as far as I could tell. Yes, there was some social segregation of black and white. All of which was voluntary. But there were plenty of ways that it was integrated. I was starting to realize that I had grown up in a bubble and that this "real world" was very, very different. After all, I can't imagine that Bob is an outlier. And there were more than enough people at Tex Mex Lex that agreed with Bob, or at the very least, had no interest in verbally disagreeing with him.

I, like almost everyone else in the place, just sat and listened to his rants throughout the day and into the evening. I spent much of the afternoon pondering the virtues of popping him. It was easy enough for me to imagine that the world had to be a better place without Bob in it. But I would always come back around to the same thing. Who am I to make that decision for the world? I know that in Jane's world there are plenty of those decisions that are necessary and clear cut. At least to her. And I guess to me as well, since I decided to accept her decisions and to do her bidding. For the moment at least, I was happy to leave those decisions to her. So for now, Bob would live to sell more trailers and eat more McDonald's.

I left at about 10 p.m. and made the long drive home before returning to his trailer at 7:30 the next morning. His truck had not left the trailer since he had arrived home at about 1 a.m. the night before.

He and Sheila emerged from the trailer at 9:10 a.m. Bob looked like he was dressed for work. Sheila looked like she was dressed for church. Which makes sense because that's exactly where they went.

The Blooming Desert Church of Christ was a modest

church by modern standards. The two of them, plus seventy or so others, wandered into the church just before the 9:30 service. I gave a little bit of thought to joining them inside. No doubt I would have been welcome. A nice white boy seeking the Lord, just like them. But I saw nothing to gain and no reason to attract attention to myself. I just did what people performing surveillance do most. Sat on my balls and waited. No misogyny intended here. I am sure there are plenty of women doing the same thing somewhere with their comparable body parts.

Ninety minutes later, the happy couple emerged from the church with the rest of the congregation. I was parked across the street but made no effort to follow. They were headed home. By the time I got there, Bob came out of the trailer now dressed in jeans and a giant plaid shirt, holding a pair of work gloves. I just drove by and let the GPS do the work. It became clear pretty quickly that he was on the interstate headed for Albuquerque. Again, I didn't follow him directly. I just started driving toward the city. Forty-five minutes later I arrived at his location. It was on the outskirts of town in a suburban area. On one side of the road were several modest homes that looked new. Most were separated by an empty lot or two. On the other side of the street were five homes in various stages of construction. There were several dozen people working on the homes. I pulled up across the street and saw Bob working a power saw, cutting wood. Behind him was a massive blue-and-green banner that read "Habitat for Humanity." The son of a bitch was doing charity work!

Just when I'd thought this guy was an unredeemable, fat, racist piece of shit, here he goes and does something a little admirable. The nerve of him.

This was the end of my surveillance work, and what an interesting ending it was. It was almost ninety minutes home from there, and I spent most of that drive brooding about the fact that I could very well have popped that guy. And there might be more to him than an annoying loudmouth. People are complicated. Situations are complicated. And it was certainly best that I don't trust my own desire to be judge, jury, and executioner. Just being obnoxious can't and shouldn't warrant a death sentence. Yes, I would perform whatever Jane asked of me. But there better be a damn good and complete reason for it. I started preparing the report as soon as I got home and sent it off to Kate and Jane Monday morning.

We were a little over ten months into my training when it began to become very specific. Motorcycles were brought in, and they would criss-cross the range two at a time from fifty to five hundred yards away. By this time, we already had the platforms and I had been shooting from at different heights to simulate targeting from building to building or building to ground level. Almost all of the work with the motorcycles was done at night. After about a month of this, it occurred to me that this must have something to do with a mission. As it turned out, I was right.

EIGHT

John's training was almost exactly as I expected. He was thorough, eager, and competent at almost everything we threw at him. And we threw a lot. The main thing, the most important thing, was his skills as a sniper. He was perfect, or as close to being perfect as can be. I got regular reports from all of his trainers and, of course, Kate. And all of his meetings with Kate were recorded for my review. One of his shooting instructors told me that John had the best natural skill set of anyone he had ever trained. And that was a lot to say. He had trained hundreds. Of course, I would never tell John this. If John has any flaws in his qualifications for this career, there would be two. First, he has never faced any real adversity in his life. He has loving parents, a stable and comfortable home life. There is no drug or alcohol abuse in his home nor in his genetics. No sexual abuse or domestic violence in his home. As far as I know he has not been bullied nor been a bully. There is no way for any of us to know how he will face dire times, situations, or consequences. Even he himself cannot know. We will find out together when it happens. And it will happen.

His other "flaw" is one that pops up in almost everyone that has served in his role. And that would be the "delusions of grandeur" of a professional and successful sniper. The belief that you are distant and untouchable, both in his conscious mind and unconsciously. I saw this in my brother when he returned from his first tour. But for him it came with guilt, grief, and pain. With John I must work to keep him grounded. It is a matter of survival. If he begins to believe he is godlike and untouchable, he will be dead soon after. In this business, the sin of hubris leads to carelessness and is punishable by death. Almost every sniper in my employ has asked me at one time or another, "Could I kill the president if it were necessary?" And the answer is, yes, of course. If history has taught us one thing, it is that anyone can be killed. But if you start to believe your own hype, the one getting killed will be you. And that is why I will never tell John that he has the best skill set his instructor has ever seen.

His dealings with Bob were quite a roller coaster ride. By all accounts the guy is an obnoxious, racist loudmouth. The fact that he did charity work threw John a curveball and caused him to reflect. He spoke extensively about it with Kate, which of course, I heard about. The experience seems to have led to his conclusion that, for the time being at least, he would depend on my judgment and not involve himself in "extracurricular" activity. Perfect! That is exactly where I need him to be. So I will not be telling John the results of our background check on Mr. Robert George Bush. Bob, it seems, was even more of a shithead than John thought. He had three arrests for domestic violence. Two against his wife Sheila and another against his daughter Shayna. According to court docs, he had beaten the shit out of his daughter after discovering she was gay. She still has an active restraining order against him. Oh, and the charity work—court ordered. I doubt this putz had ever lifted a finger to help anyone.

There is no upside to John knowing any of this. It would

just confuse him. Let us not forget he is still a young man. But this young man was ready for action. His first assignment would be a particularly challenging one and that was not a coincidence. In a way it was more a test of his capacity for humility. My sniper expert instructors had assured me that this mission was so difficult that it was a virtual certainty that John would miss at least once and probably more. We will find out how he reacts to that. And it will help to keep him grounded and motivated.

Meanwhile, much of Manhattan was being deprived of sleep by a coordinated attack of extremely loud motorcycles roaming the streets between 2 and 5 a.m. Estimates suggest that close to a million people were being harmed. Our own intelligence finally reached the conclusion that this was a coordinated act of "soft terrorism." Although we didn't know the source, John would put an end to it.

I informed him that he had his first assignment. We instructed him to drive to New York. We set him up in a rental near Times Square on the third floor. Which should be a prime spot. It was still a ridiculously tough assignment, even for him. A moving motorcycle at night was about as tough as it gets, other than the fact that there were no obstruction issues.

The apartment would be fully stocked with hardware when he arrives. He was to spend two or three days getting comfortable and observing his surroundings before preparing for the shots. My beloved nephew was ready to graduate. There would be no party.

NINE

New York City. I had never been there, and I was a bit excited. After a lifetime of Army bases, Podunk towns, and Bumfuck, New Mexico, New York would be a whole new world for me. I arrived without incident and easily found my new home. Which was on the third floor of a twenty-floor apartment building in midtown, just a couple of blocks from Times Square. I spent my first day walking the streets in a touristy type of way. I tried a New York pretzel, and it was awesome. I tried my first slice of real New York pizza, and it was pretty damn good but not quite worth all the hype. I wandered Chinatown and wondered who exactly ate the pig intestines hanging in every window.

My apartment was not glamorous, but it was fine. It had a small balcony that became pitch black at night if I didn't turn on a light. Which is exactly what I needed. Aunt Jane had done her homework.

I inspected the hardware that was already there when I arrived. It was exactly what I'd asked for. I had the three weapons I felt most confident and comfortable with. There were also night vision goggles, but I didn't think I would need them. If I kept my apartment completely dark, the streetlights should offer me a sufficient view.

The next morning, I headed downstairs. There was a coffee shop in the lobby of my building that also fronted the street. It wasn't too crowded and there were only three people in front of me in line. But it did give me a chance to get a good look at the woman behind the counter. She was a tall dirty blonde, about my age. Perhaps a couple years older. She wasn't drop dead gorgeous, but she was more than pretty enough. What got me were her eyes. They weren't quite blue, more like a greenish blue. But they had an intelligence that almost always seemed to carry over to actual intelligence. She had the name "Linda" written on her name tag. I thought I saw her glance over at me once or twice while I was waiting, but it might have just been wishful thinking on my part.

When it was my turn, I started to order when she interrupted. "Drug dealer, quarterback, or trust-fund baby?" she asked. "This neighborhood costs a small fortune, and you are too young to be a rich neurosurgeon, so it has to be one of the other three, so which is it?"

"I'm new around here, so I didn't realize that there was a questionnaire to get a cup of coffee. But if you must know, I'm a rookie quarterback for the New York Jets, which means by the next time you see me I'll probably be injured."

"Nope, not buying it, you're too small for a quarterback. So, how's the fentanyl business? Let me guess, your customers are rude and keep dying on you."

I was undeterred. "Listen, Linda," I said squinting at her name tag, even though I had clearly already seen it. "What would it take to get an actual cup of coffee out of you?"

"Not much," she replied. "Just your undying love, your phone number, and nine bucks. Welcome to New York."

"Hmm," I replied. "I can do the undying love and the digits, but the nine bucks is a bit of a stretch on a drug dealer's salary.

Besides, there's now about thirteen angry New Yorkers behind me in line. I'd hate to get beat up on my first day in New York, so make me a large cup of regular coffee, sugar only, and I'll comply with your other demands."

She was laughing as she made the coffee and talking out loud to herself. "No espresso, no cappuccino, no milkshakes. This one's a weirdo."

"You have no idea," I replied.

I picked up a magic marker off the counter and wrote my number on a twenty-dollar bill. I handed it to her when she gave me the coffee. "Keep the change . . . and I bet you never call me," I said as I made my way past the increasingly annoyed line and out to the street.

I really was like a wide-eyed kid in the big city. It's just weird for someone like me seeing that many people in the same place. Throngs of people crossing the intersections and on their way somewhere. But what really struck me was how fat almost everybody was. Again, in my little military bubble, there weren't a ton of truly fat people. Sure, there were plenty of people who were overweight, but nothing even close to this "general public" I was now seeing. All the more remarkable in that New York is a city where people do a lot of walking and bike riding. How in the world could so many people be so fucking fat?

And because I'm me I spent a good part of that evening researching the subject. The average weight of Americans has skyrocketed over the last fifty years. Portion sizes, increased fat and sugar intake, and the rise of "fast food" have all played a role. Sixty-five percent of adults and thirty percent of kids are seriously overweight or obese. Holy shit! Even our plates are bigger than they used to be. But the bigger picture seemed to show that the government is subsidizing (with our tax dollars, of course) the things that make us fat. The biggest culprit being corn and the derived corn syrup, which is in almost everything.

Even worse, the epidemic of fat was, as usual, hurting the poor way more than the rich. The poor had way less access to healthy foods for reasons both of price and location. This all made a lot of rich people get healthy and richer but gave the poor an even heavier burden to carry, literally.

This shit is part of the reason I don't get invited to a lot of parties. Things like this interest me. But the bottom line is we have become a fat, sick, diabetic country. And the costs are more than just bigger clothes. Billions are spent on healthcare to take care of these folks and the government doesn't seem to care. Or they're just too busy taking money from the giant food corporations to notice. This is actually a threat to national security. One that I hope Aunt Jane understands.

That afternoon I took a long nap so I could be alert for the early morning hours. The buzzing of Manhattan had been occurring virtually every night, but my plan for tonight was just to observe.

At about 10 p.m. I got a text from Linda, "You were right, I didn't call," to which I answered, "There's nothing hotter than a woman who keeps her word."

We texted back and forth for a couple of hours. She said she was a graduate student in psychology at NYU. She said she had a bunch of student loans and worked at the coffee shop part time for spending money. I couldn't figure out what to tell her about myself. It occurred to me that maybe it should have been part of my training. Some type of cover story for anyone I may encounter. So, I told her she'd been right. I was indeed a trust-fund baby and a tourist. I was spending a year just traveling and trying to "find myself" and what I wanted to do with my life. I figured if I really got to know her, I could be fairly honest about my youth spent around the Army. I would just say that the family fortune had something to do with defense contracts or some such nonsense. Never lie when the truth will do.

It had been about a year since I'd had a girlfriend, and I

wasn't exactly looking for one. Especially since I was about to perform my first assignment. But this girl was really cool. She was pretty, certainly not shy, and seemed to be able to converse about anything. Even though it was just texting, it seemed to flow smoothly without any awkward pauses.

Again, it was Linda who made the first move when she texted, "Well, you passed the first test."

When I asked what that meant, she replied with, "We've been texting back and forth for two hours, and you haven't asked for a photo of my tits or sent me a dick pic." It's almost certain that Jane, and probably Kate could see everything on my phone. Not that I would ever send anyone a dick pic, but I couldn't help but laugh at the thought of the two of them combing through my texts to assess my state of mind and my dick.

I replied that I hadn't realized the bar was so low, that I had passed her "test" just by not being a complete asshole.

"You'd be surprised," she replied.

"The Dick Pic has become the modern equivalent of saying good morning!" And then she sent me a picture of some tits. Clearly not her tits, but tits. I had to stop myself from laughing loud enough to wake up my neighbors as I sat on my balcony at 1 a.m.

"OK," I replied. "I didn't know I had a test, but you just passed it! What do we do now, how about lunch tomorrow?"

This was my not-completely-absent male ego kicking in. I figured I had to be something other than completely passive and see if she wanted to go the next step with me. I was happy when her response came back, "Sure! Why not. How does two sound? I'll text you the place. It'll be somewhere close by."

That got me thinking a little bit. Close by? How did she know that I was staying in that building? But before I could decide if I was going to ask, she followed up with "You're staying in that building, right? Most of the people that come into the coffee shop do."

"Yes," I replied. "And If you're a really good girl you might get to see my glamorous apartment before I leave."

She replied with a sarcastic emoji and, "Hmmm, I don't know if I can ever be quite good enough for a man with your overwhelming charm and lack of dick pics. . . . My goodness, I do believe I feel one of my spells coming on." She followed that up with three rather explicit photos that, again, were definitely not her.

"Well, I think it's best you lay down for a bit until it passes. I think I'm going to bed, alone and lonely. Do you feel sorry for me?"

"No," she replied. "But I will see you tomorrow at two. Don't be late or I'll kill ya."

"Text me the place and I'll be there. Hey, this was fun. I'll see you tomorrow."

By now it was almost 2 a.m. It wasn't long before I heard the first of what was probably three or four loud motorcycles roaming the streets. From the noise, I suspected they were separate and their goal was to cover and disrupt as large of an area as possible. One of them buzzed past my window about five minutes later and it was incredibly loud. I'm a pretty sound sleeper, but I was quite sure that it would have been more than loud enough to wake me up. My thoughts were confirmed as I began to see lights come on in the building across the street.

Over the next two hours, the buzzing stopped and started again several times. I saw at least three or four different bikes and riders. They were dressed in all black and wore black helmets. But there were enough differences for me to tell they weren't all the same person. My instructions were to take out two of them in the same night as quickly as possible. But I had already decided to myself that one would do if it would be risky to get the second. I was confident, perhaps even overconfident, that I could make the shots cleanly from my balcony without being seen or heard.

I didn't know it, but Jane had rented the apartments on both sides of mine. The weapons I used with the silencers I was provided were quiet, but they weren't absolutely silent. The sound was not unlike that of the suction devices they use at bank drive-thrus. Unless they were expert, anyone hearing the shots wouldn't even realize they were hearing gunfire. Not to mention the sounds of the bikes themselves drowning out the gunshots. I was ready for my mission. I texted a single word to Jane, "Ready."

Linda had texted me directions to a diner just two blocks away. I got there about ten minutes early and sat in a booth. I don't know why, but I expected it to look like the diner on *Seinfeld*. It didn't. But it was a nice enough place with a massive menu. They had dishes from Greek to Chinese and more or less everything else. Linda showed up right on time and looked, well, great. She wasn't dressed in anything special, just jeans and a T-shirt. But you could see much more of her than you could see under the apron at the coffee shop, and I very much liked what I was seeing. She just slid into the booth opposite me and started talking as if continuing our text chat from the night before.

"What's for lunch, John?" she asked, opening the huge menu.

"I haven't given it much thought," I said. "My mind has been completely preoccupied with thoughts of you." I'd said it with a hint of sarcasm, but in reality, it wasn't that far from the truth. Especially the way she looked today.

She looked at me over the menu and said, "Wow, that's some strong game there, John. It almost worries me how good that sounded. Almost like you say it to every coffee-slinging girl you might meet."

"Need I remind you, Madam, of whom is gaming whom. I don't remember asking you for your phone number ..."

"True," she interrupted. "But you did ask me to lunch." Any hint of sarcasm faded away as she said, "And I am really glad you did."

Those words washed over me like a warm breeze on a cold night. It's true. I'm not capable of feeling love in the way most people are. But at that moment, I liked the living fuck out of this woman.

A heartfelt, "I'm glad I did too," was the best response I could come up with.

We ate and sat and talked for over two hours. She was born and raised on Long Island and had moved into the city for college. She had a bachelor's in psychology and was working, mostly online, for her masters. She lived just a couple of blocks away in a three-bedroom apartment with two roommates. Both of which were gay flight attendants and the best roommates imaginable because they were almost never there. And when they were actually there, they were usually sleeping.

I tried my best to tell her the truth of my life spent mostly on and around Army bases. Of my formal education or lack thereof. I told her I was interested in everything and nothing, which is about as truthful as I can be. We shared some overlapping interests. She came off as curious and bright, not a genius by any stretch but smarter than most and not driven by the mundane world of social media and celebrity. In fact, and I would have to ask Kate about what this meant, she was sort of a female version of me in a lot of ways.

She asked me a question and I could tell by her tone that my answer was important. "*Star Trek* or *Star Wars*?"

"I like both," I answered, but she cut me off before I could explain.

"Don't be wishy-washy, John. It's a simple question. *Star Trek* or *Star Wars*?"

"*Star Trek*," I finally admitted. "Mostly because *Star Wars* was like two good movies and then a bunch of crap. I haven't watched a ton of *Star Trek*, but most of what I've seen I liked. It's optimistic, at least."

Linda looked relieved. "I'm not a huge fan of either, myself, but *Star Wars* is just so fucking dumb. And I think you're right, *Star Trek* at least manages to show us that we can be better than the ridiculous dipshits we are now. Thank god! I don't think I could date a *Star Wars* fan, even if he looked like Bradley Cooper and was hung like a horse."

I looked across at her after that speech and replied with a laugh, "You know, I think it's best if you try to express your true feelings and not keep things so bottled up inside. It's not good for you." We both laughed and I added, "OK, I guess I passed the second test. No dick pics, check. No *Star Wars*, check. Oh, and are we dating?"

"I think so," she answered, "or else what have we been doing for the last two hours?"

"Definitely not watching *Star Wars*!" I said, and again we were laughing. I liked her laugh a lot. I liked her a lot.

Soon I was walking her home through the crowded rush-hour streets.

"This is me," she said with a gesture to the building behind her.

I leaned in and gave her a soft kiss on the cheek. There was no attempt to move away on her part.

"Thanks for lunch," she said.

"My pleasure," I replied. "Maybe dinner next time?" I asked and gave her another soft kiss.

"I'm not sure," she said with a wry smile. "Text me. You never know."

And just like that she was gone. I was definitely going to text her. But I had some business to attend to that night.

I went back to the apartment and went straight to sleep. I

wanted to be fresh when it was time to work. I woke to the alarm at 1 a.m. and began preparing the equipment while I made coffee. By 2 a.m. I was on the balcony with all the lights in my apartment off. There was more than enough light from streetlights and a half moon. It wasn't long before I heard the scream of the motorcycles in the distance. My entire life had led up to this moment. When push comes to shove, could I take the shots? Could I take a life?

Well, yes, I took the shots. But I took no lives. Over a two-hour period I discharged my weapon seven times. The good news: I didn't attract any attention or wake anybody up. The bad news: I missed every shot.

I reported to Jane with a single word, "Nope." I would explain later.

I spent the rest of that morning trying to figure out how I'd missed. For a while I decided I was going to blame the thin rubber gloves I was wearing. But that was bullshit. I had trained for at least a hundred hours gloved. The thought occurred to me that in two hours I had already missed more than my father had missed in his entire career. Beating myself up wasn't going to help me hit the targets. So I forced myself to stop and show myself a bit of empathy. A psychological technique that had been well taught to me by Kate. The truth is these were incredibly tough targets. There probably aren't a hundred people on the planet that could perform this assignment. And apparently, I wasn't one of them yet. But I was determined that I would be.

I stayed in the apartment all day and forced myself to stay awake until 5 p.m. and again set my alarm for 1 a.m. I performed the same ritual of coffee and preparation and again sat alone on a darkened balcony and awaited my prey.

My first shot passed through the neck of the first biker at 3:10 a.m., the second just five minutes later as the second biker had come to check on the first. In the street there were now two dead bikers, two wrecked bikes, and not yet any sirens or police lights. I brought everything in from the balcony in quiet darkness. Almost as if on cue, I heard and saw the approach of the police just as I closed the door to the balcony.

Then I laid down quietly in the darkness and again texted Jane a single word, "Done."

I stayed there, awake until the sun rose. I hadn't even looked out over the balcony as the bodies and wreckage were taken away. There was no reason to risk being seen on the balcony. But I was in no danger of being discovered. There were hundreds of apartments that the shots could have come from. I saw on the TV later that afternoon that the police had declared both deaths to have been caused by motorcycle crashes, with the second wreck occurring by crashing into the first. This may very well have been the result of influence from Aunt Jane, or perhaps not. I never asked. My first mission was complete, and I was none the worse for wear. My confidence had been briefly shaken but returned with the two perfect shots. I was to remain in the apartment for two more days before moving on to another assignment. Instructions were pending.

I hadn't texted Linda in a day and a half, so I texted her a single word, "Dinner?"

It occurred to me that Linda might expect an explanation of my absence, especially since our first date had gone so well. At least I'd thought so.

She replied with "Sure! Tonight seven p.m., I'll text you the place," and then followed up with "playas gonna play."

It wasn't a demand for an explanation as much as her own explanation. That I was "playing games" by waiting so as not to seem overeager. That will do, I thought to myself. But the truth is I would've texted her immediately had I not had business to attend to. I wasn't thinking too far ahead, but I started to wonder about what will happen when I leave. Could I possibly maintain any kind of relationship with her? I already knew I wanted one. But it was difficult to imagine what that might look like.

She texted later, asking me to meet her in front of her building. This time she wore a dress. She looked amazing. I had no idea what to expect in terms of where we were going, and I didn't asked. It ended up being a fairly long walk to a simple family-style Italian restaurant. It's New York City, so it was still crazy expensive, but it wasn't a fancy place. A pretty typical red-and-white-checkered-tablecloth type of restaurant with really good food.

Again, we sat across from each other in a booth and the conversation continued as if there hadn't been two days in between. We ended up sharing two bottles of a red wine she'd chosen. I know next to nothing about wine and don't drink it often, but this was a tasty little bugger, and I caught the slightest bit of a buzz from it, as I'm sure she must have as well. We spilled back onto the street with her subtly taking the lead, walking back toward her building.

"You know I'm not gonna fuck you," she said matter-of-factly. "At least not anytime soon."

I had started to become accustomed to her very particular style of bluntness, but that was a bit much, even for her. I was trying to come up with some kind of witty response, but it was too late as she continued, "But if you want to come up and not watch *Star Wars* with me you are more than welcome. Just don't expect to be laying all over me." I didn't respond for over a minute as we kept walking and approached the entrance to her building. "Sure," I finally said, and we headed upstairs.

There was a certain amount of irony in the fact that a half hour later I was indeed "laying all over her." But we remained more or less fully clothed and more than a little breathless. We kissed, we touched, and we explored each other, but I remained respectful. I wasn't asking for an explanation, but she offered one anyway. "I like sex as much as anybody, maybe more," she said. "But I like you and I want to see if this might become about something more than that."

We sat on the couch together at this point, knee to knee, and I said, "So does that mean if you didn't like me, we'd be fucking right now?"

"No, dipshit," she laughed. "If I didn't like you, you wouldn't be here at all."

I found that answer to be perfectly satisfactory and, to tell the truth, part of me was glad that we weren't going to go "all the way." Don't get me wrong, I wanted to. I really wanted to. But this was good. And it would give me a reason to find my way back to her once I left. If she would have me.

The next night was my last in New York City. I had my marching orders, and I was headed upstate, about a four-hour drive north for what Jane described as "an easier assignment." Some might take that as a subtle dig for having missed on my first night. But I chose not to take it that way. I saw it as more of an acknowledgement of just how difficult that first mission was and her appreciation that I had completed it. I could be wrong, but that was another bit of Kate programming kicking in. Look for the positive in what others had to offer. Why not?

Linda worked that day and told me she was pissed at me because she got up at 6 a.m. for work. I hadn't left her apartment, quite hesitantly, until well after 1 a.m. She was tired and so I went straight to her apartment. We ordered dinner delivered and again failed to watch *Star Wars*.

She didn't seem surprised when I told her I was leaving the next day. I had to go upstate, I told her truthfully. To see some family, I lied. I had no idea where I would be beyond the next four days so there was nothing I could tell her about coming back. Something I very much wanted to do. She didn't question me. We just enjoyed each other's company and not having sex. But coming dangerously close from time to time.

"I will see you soon, if you'll let me," I said as I was leaving.

"No bullshit, John, I would really like that. But, hey, it's not like you're going to the moon. We'll stay in touch. . . . You aren't going to the moon, right?"

"Only if you're there," I answered as we shared one last embrace.

TEN

Jane had switched out my vehicle and delivered a different one that was unlocked by an app on my phone. The keys were inside. Something about that made me feel like this official spy guy for some reason. It was more than a four-hour drive north to the small town of Allset. Jane had asked me to call her when I got on the highway. It occurred to me that I couldn't remember the last time we had spoken on the phone. Almost all our communications were through text. I had the sense that she wanted to hear my voice as part of her assessment of my state of mind after my first assignment.

The fact is that I had just murdered two people. Whether they deserved it was almost beside the point. I'm sure Jane wanted to know if that had affected me. The truth was that it hadn't affected me at all. Not in any way I could tell. It really had just been a job, a technical issue to be completed. Truthfully, I felt nothing more than satisfaction. Subconsciously, of course, was another matter and probably one best left for Kate to unravel.

I was one hundred percent certain that Jane and Kate knew of my time with Linda. Definitely from my text messages and perhaps even active surveillance. I was under no illusions that anything I did would escape their notice. So, I felt prepared to discuss anything and everything with my boss as I dialed her number.

"Did you get laid?" she asked before even saying hello.

I wasn't surprised and, since I was hoping to get a chance to get back to New York City, I answered, "Not yet, but I sure as shit am going to try. Which leads me to the question: Am I going to get back to New York City anytime soon? I really do want to see her."

"Look, John," Jane answered, "I have no problem with these kinds of extracurricular activities, as long as they don't distract you from your work. I know you told her you were a trust-fund baby, so that gives you a bit of flexibility. I've been working on your schedule and, after Allset, you'll have a couple more quick missions in Upstate New York and then you can go back to the city. I'm guessing that could be as soon as a week or two. So you can tell her that."

"Thanks, Jane," I replied. "So tell me about the next mission. Who are we popping and why?"

She hesitated for a moment as if she were deciding whether to discuss it with me.

"This will be among the most important missions you will ever perform. It won't be a difficult one, but it is incredibly important and a little sticky in terms of who he is and the connections he has. This asshole Forrest Reagan is the most dangerous white supremacist in history. At his lab in Allset, he's overseeing the creation of a virus that will kill or render sterile every black person in existence. He's so sick he makes us seem normal by comparison."

"Well, I can't argue with this assignment. I promise it will be clean and quick."

Jane replied, "Thank you, but let's get one thing clear. I won't always be able provide a detailed reason for every mission, nor should you expect one. Give me about five minutes and I will help you to understand why."

"Go ahead, AJ, it's not like I don't have the time."

She seemed to go into teacher mode as she began, "The year 2003 was one of the most important in human history and hardly anybody even noticed. And before I go on, I want you to know that no matter how outrageous it may sound, everything I am about to tell you is the absolute truth. Yes, there might be some small variations based on our actions as a species going forward. But as we sit here tonight. It is the absolute truth."

While she spoke, I got the sense that I had just now "graduated." Since I completed my first mission, I was now one of them. And these were some of the things I needed to know.

"So, in 2003, two things happened. First, climate change became irreversible. In less than a century, probably less, about a third of places where people live will be uninhabitable. Of those areas, many will simply be under water. Others will become uninhabitable due to drought, excessive rain, temperature, fires, or something of the like."

A dazed "Wow!" was the only response I could muster. Like most people, I thought we still had time. Maybe not the will, but certainly some time. Scientists continue to tell us that we can fix it if we act now. But I was beginning to suspect that it was mostly PR and a desire just to prevent even worse consequences.

"The second and even more profound thing is this," she continued. "In 2003, we passed a threshold. Technology made it possible for us to have the resources to cloth, house, and feed every person in the world. This is true and will remain true even in the world I just described under the effects of climate change."

"All we lack to make that a reality is the collective human

will to do so. And it is incredibly difficult to even imagine a political scenario that brings it about. But that doesn't mean we shouldn't try."

I interrupted at this point, "Is this our real mission, AJ? Are we here to try to create some kind of economic heaven on earth?"

"Not exactly," she said. "Our first duty is always to the good old U.S. of A. But it's always in the back of my mind. It might take decades. Hell, it may never happen. But isn't that something worth working for?"

I laughed just a little, but that was enough for her to ask, "What the fuck is so funny?"

"I don't know," I answered. "If there were some kind of record or award for irony, I think we would win the trophy. Two murderous sociopaths plotting an eventual heaven on earth. What's stopping us?"

"More things than I can count. From politics to religion to plain old human nature. But there is one thing in particular. Have you ever heard of the group Creating Real American Progress?"

"No," I admitted, and I started laughing again.

"Yes, you fucken toddler. It spells out CRAP, but this is no joke. This group is a conglomeration of the world's largest and most powerful corporations. And the thing to remember here, John, is that there is no such thing as an American company anymore. The people who own the world's largest and most powerful companies are mostly foreigners, hedge funds, and mutual funds. None of whom owe any allegiance to the United States or any other country. They couldn't give two shits about our jobs, our lives, our infrastructure, or anything else. So CRAP works out of Bentonville, Arkansas, and has inflicted more harm on the US public than any war ever has. They're eating us alive from the inside out. Their main purpose is to write actual legislation on hundreds of different topics. But all the law they write and mastermind are strictly for their own benefit. They then hand them to lawmakers at every level. More often than not, their bills get passed, often verbatim and unread by the politicians who are bought and paid for. And even if an elected lawmaker disagrees or is not outright corrupt, he will go along with it anyway. Because if they don't, their political careers are over. With very few exceptions, any lawmaker can lose reelection with a few million dollars passed to their opponent either in the primary or general election. They destroy environmental protections, raise barriers of entry to protect their monopolies and duopolies that have done immeasurable harm to Americans. . . . The list of shit is so long that you would be halfway through Canada by the time I get done telling you."

I listened very carefully as she spoke and not just because she's my boss. What she was telling me was something that I felt like I already understood on a molecular level as an enthusiastic but informal student of economics. It didn't take much awareness to notice that America's middle class has all but disappeared. You would have to be blind to not notice that the basics of life—food, shelter, healthcare, and education—have become incredibly expensive, far beyond the rate of inflation. What used to be known as a normal middle-class life was now out of reach for untold millions of Americans.

"So why don't we just start popping them, AJ? It may not fix everything, but it would certainly be a step in the right direction."

"Because it would be like declaring war," answered Jane. "A war we are not ready to win. Look, John, I believe in capitalism and free markets, and I bet you do too. But what we have now is corporate oligarchy and corruption. The exact antithesis of democratic capitalism. You grew up in the single most successful socialist organization in the world, the US military. They're provided food, clothing, housing, and even once they're out, they get free healthcare for life. There is absolutely no reason that everyone can't have that . . . if we want it. Only then can this child species take any steps toward safety and maturity.

"I have a thought assignment for you and Kate if you want to include her. I want you to try to imagine a world where every single human is assured food, water, shelter, and education as a birthright. Really think about it. It is a difference so vast that, like me, it will take you months to even to begin to understand. Run it past Kate. It will be helpful to get a female perspective. Now, get your ass to Allset and pop that piece of shit. And, John, that was good work in New York. A million people will sleep tonight because of you."

She hung up. This was starting to become a habit of hers. Dumping giant issues, questions, and thoughts in my head then leaving me to think about it. Well, I still had three hours to Allset. I might as well get started.

I called Kate, who answered with, "So you got Jane's heaven on earth speech?"

Again, I wasn't surprised. I was getting used to the fact that I would have these two women in my head all the time.

"Yeah," I said with a soft chuckle. "I didn't realize she was such a commie."

"Not a commie," Kate replied. "She's probably the furthest thing from a communist that you could possibly imagine. Free markets are the reason so many people have lived so well for so long. Capitalism has raised more people out of poverty than any other economic system in history. But let me ask you something. If I'm not mistaken, if you live in any state other than Texas there is exactly one company you can buy electricity from. Is that a free market?"

It's something I never thought about before. After all, I have never even paid an electric bill.

"Of course not," I answered, "but I assume they're regulated by someone at the state level."

Now it was her turn to laugh. "Really? On one side you have a multibillion-dollar monopoly and on the other you have some schleps on a state energy board or council that is supposed to regulate them. It's a joke. In reality, these companies have a blank check and can charge whatever they want. Now try this one. When you walk into a McDonald's, what do you suppose the guy at the counter makes?"

"I don't know," I answered. "About ten dollars an hour. Hey, I thought you were my therapist, not an economics teacher."

She ignored my comment and continued, "OK, let's say they make twelve dollars an hour. Four hundred eighty a week before taxes, and that's if they are lucky enough to get full-time hours. So, for argument's sake, let's say they take home sixteen hundred a month. There is no way even a single person can live on that, let alone a couple or a family, so how do they survive?"

"I don't know," I replied. "Food stamps, welfare?"

"Exactly!" Kate responded. "And who do you suppose pays for that—don't answer, we both know—taxpayers. It's taxpayers who pay the difference. So, without getting too far into the weeds here, what you have is socialism of the worst kind. We pay their employees, and they make the profit. And it's not just McDonald's. Ask yourself, why should we pay their employees and they make the profit? That's not capitalism. It's not free markets. It's reverse capitalism. And they can pull it off because they are so huge and so powerful that they can make us pay their employees even if we never set foot in one of their stores."

I'm not the sharpest tool in the shed, but I know when I'm being manipulated. This set of conversations with these women in my life was not incidental. They had a specific purpose. Not that I minded. When you get right down to it, there was nothing here I didn't already know. I'd just never really taken the time to think about it. The seed had been well planted. I began to see the tentacles of corporate oligarchy everywhere I looked.

They wanted me to start getting a look at the big picture. And I did. But there was work to be done in Allset, and I was almost there.

ELEVEN

I checked into my room at the Hope Springs Casino at Allset. It was operated by the indigenous Nonya tribe on their own land. The laboratory was also on Indian land, but it was operated by a company I had never heard of called Geneworks. They were a biotech startup supposedly with a contract with the Department of Defense. For this mission I'd brought along my own equipment, a single weapon that was carried in three parts in my lone suitcase. It would be a daytime shot of close to three quarters of a mile. There wouldn't be any more sophisticated equipment required.

The room was on the fifth floor, which was at the top of this relatively small hotel. It also had an almost completely enclosed balcony. I found out later that it is unusual for casino hotels to have balconies or even unlocked windows. Apparently some people would toss themselves out of the hotel windows after losing all their money.

I had the room for three nights, but I probably wouldn't need it. There was a clear sightline from my balcony to the steps of the laboratory three quarters of a mile away. I had good pictures of the soon-to-be-departed Forrest Reagan. I was told that you could set your watch by the guy. That he climbed those steps every weekday morning at precisely 8:30 a.m. Steps were the best place to take out a walking target. A target walking on level ground is less predictable. They may slow, stop, turn around, or find a quarter on the ground. A person climbing steps will move up in a steady and predictable way and they're less likely to be distracted.

Tomorrow morning, I will use the scope of my rifle to observe him as he goes into the building. Just to make sure I'm getting the right guy. The next morning, I will decorate the steps with some white supremacist brains.

I had been texting with Linda almost constantly. She didn't ask too much about what I was doing. Which was nice because I didn't need to do a lot of lying. She was working a lot, studying and doing a lot of hinting that she could use a vacation. Preferably someplace warmer than New York. "Florida sounds pretty nice this time of year baby, ya think?" Subtle she was not. And I had replied that a little trip together might be just what the doctor ordered. But I was booked up for the time being.

I had no problem spotting Forrest the next morning as he climbed the stairs, holding only a satchel. I briefly flirted with the idea of popping him just to get it over with. But I was determined not to miss this time. There was no need to rush. I spent most of the rest of the day getting a little exercise. A light workout in the hotel gym followed by a five-mile jog in a hoodie. I wasn't hiding, but I spent no time on the casino floor. Not that there was much concern. But Jane had warned me that there were hundreds of surveillance cameras in every casino. There was no need to be a smart ass.

It had become almost a ritual for me. I set my alarm for 7:30 a.m. I got up, started the coffee, and assembled my weapon. In this instance I would be leaving immediately after the shot, so I prepared my suitcase. I would only need to disassemble the weapon, pack it, and haul my butt on out of there. It's not that there would be much worry of being caught. The target was three quarters of a mile away and it would take time for them to figure out where the shot came from. I would be gone in the ensuing chaos. It was more than likely that they would never determine exactly where the shot came from.

My aim was true. For the first time I could see my victim's head explode. But I didn't dwell on what I had seen and was in the car and off the property in less than five minutes. The only instruction I had was to head north. Again, I texted Jane a single word, "Done." A minute later I received a text from Jane with the information for a hotel in Troy, New York. It was about an hour away. I stopped for breakfast then made my way to the hotel to await further instructions.

"We're going to clean up the drug trade in the Capital District, John," said Jane on the phone with her usual aversion to saying "hello" or any other greeting. She just hit the ground running, as always. "What the fuck is the Capital District, AJ, and who or what am I supposed to clean up?"

"The Capital District is the city of Troy, where you are now, plus Schenectady and Albany, which is the actual state capital. It's kind of one big city. There are six people that control almost all of the drug trade in the zone, and I'm going to send you info on five of them. One will live to tell the tale." I was about to ask why, when she continued, "These morons have been adding fentanyl to almost every street drug like somebody putting salt on a baked potato. People are dropping dead left and right because that shit is potent, and they don't know what they're doing."

Again, I was about to interject but as usual she anticipated my question. "I know, other people will take over the business but in the meantime, there will be chaos and a disruption to the flow. So we're likely to save a bunch of lives worth saving. Imagine, you think you're buying an eight ball of coke for the weekend and you and your friends end up dead. We aren't saving Boy Scouts here, but it's out of control. You will bring it under control."

"Um, can I say something now?" I asked hopefully. "Jesus, AJ, I get it, but take a breath once in a while."

But she barely slowed down. "You've got a week to pop all five. But I recommend you do plenty of recon first and then pop them all the same day, or two days max, because once you start, the others might drop out of sight. You will have seven different apartments to work from. That will get you clear shots at all of them. I will send you all the intel you need for targets and locations. And when you're done you can go back to the city and see your girlfriend. So hopefully that inspires you."

I started to protest that Linda wasn't my girlfriend when I realized Jane had hung up. At the same time my phone buzzed with a text. Jane, of course. "I almost forgot, any problem with what you saw on the steps?" That was her way of asking if I had been affected by watching Forrest's head explode.

"No," I replied. "But thanks for asking." I hoped she could sense the sarcasm of my reply, but knowing her it wouldn't matter even if she did.

But she was right. I was inspired. I spent three days doing reconnaissance and then got all but one of them on the fourth day. The fifth I got the next morning. I had the sense that these five assassinations were something of a luxury for Jane. These weren't world-changing hits. Drugs would be harder to get for a while and hopefully whoever replaced them would be smart enough to not keep killing their customers. But that was no sure thing. I could easily imagine being back here in six months cleaning house again. I thought I had earned a vacation, but no such luck. As I drove back to New York City, I began to get info from Jane on new targets and locations. All in the city. There were four total, and they had one thing in common: all were Saudi nationals.

This whole thing was going to be a completely different kind of project. First, she wanted them all done at once. That alone presented all kinds of potential problems. You hit one, maybe two and then they realize it and start to scatter. So three and four will be panicked, moving targets. The weapon I was to use in the city was Russian, and I was to leave it at the site to be found. I had no problem with this model of Russian-made sniper rifle. I'd practiced with it plenty back in New Mexico. But it would never be my first choice. Obviously, there was a political reason, but Jane was not forthcoming, and I thought it best to save those questions for after the mission. This was going to be a big deal. There would be no sweeping it under the rug and Jane knew it. I was going to kill four Saudi nationals affiliated with their embassy just a couple of blocks from the U.N. And I was going to use a Russian-made weapon to boot.

They would know where the shots came from, and they would find the weapon. That means that, for the first time, they'd have something to potentially find and identify me.

I would not set foot in the apartment I was to shoot from until minutes before the shots, and I would need to get out immediately and leave the weapon behind.

I had two days in New York City before the mission. I was happy to see Linda and she was happy to see me. But, to be honest, I was nervous about this mission. For some reason this somehow made it all real to me. My prior assignments had felt safe to me, detached. This one was different. It was clearly a set of politically motivated, public assassinations in broad daylight. There was nothing clean or safe about it. But, as Jane reminded me, I was never promised safe or clean.

I called Kate. Obviously, we couldn't discuss details, but she seemed to know about the mission. Or perhaps she just knew that there would be missions like these. She listened patiently as any good therapist would. She offered only that I had been well trained for my work. And that I would not have received the assignment if I was not ready. This was surprisingly reassuring.

And then she added something unexpected. "You have someone to live for, John, and something. That's more than most people ever get."

Damn, she was good at this! It's as if she had crawled in my head and told me exactly what I needed to hear.

I spent most of the next day with Linda. And it just so happened that we took a walk that included the street near the U.N. where I would be working the next day. Later, I went alone to the apartment I would be working from, but only for a couple of minutes. I just needed to make sure that I had enough familiarity with the place to get in and out quickly.

I think Linda could sense the difference in me. I tried my best, but she was too smart to not notice that I was a little distant, a little preoccupied.

We had dinner at the same diner where we'd had our first date. But I didn't return to her apartment, despite her invitation. I told her I wasn't feeling well and that I would see her tomorrow. I think I knew when I said it that it wasn't true. The only thing I could hope for was that she wouldn't be too put off by my behavior. It wasn't like I'd been completely different. But we both knew that I would normally jump at the chance to go back to her place.

I was to be at the apartment at 4 p.m. I was told that the targets would appear on the street between 4:15 and 4:30. I was in place and ready. Jane knew the difficulty of four almost simultaneous hits. So she had given me a priority order in case I couldn't get all of them, I would get the most important targets first.

I had the first of them in my sights. My finger tensed on the trigger. Suddenly I felt something cold on the back of my neck. It was the unmistakable cold steel of a gun. How could this happen? How could I have left the door unlocked? How did I not hear him come in? How could I be so horribly, fatally careless?

"Take your finger off the trigger," said a faceless accented voice. I did as I was told. "Place the weapon on the table, slowly," he said, the gun still pressed to the back of my neck.

He's an amateur, I thought to myself. Or a professional as careless as me. He should have known enough to put some distance between us. But he didn't and it was now or never. I placed the weapon on the table as instructed. But I spun quickly with my right arm at shoulder height. The idea was to move his weapon from its threatening position. I didn't expect it to work. I anticipated the blackness of death. But instead, my elbow met his arm just below his elbow. He still held the weapon, but his body was turned to me and out of position to fire. I took advantage and jumped at him, bringing my chest to his shoulder from the side. We both fell to the ground with me on top. The gun had fallen from his grasp. I landed a sloppy but hard blow to the side of his face. He was even more dazed after the back of his head hit the hardwood floor. Again, I took advantage and sat astride him, punching repeatedly until my hands hurt and I was sure he was unconscious.

Quickly I returned to my weapon and the window, finding my targets still on the street. There was no time to think as I squeezed off my first and second shot. I hit both targets, killing them instantly. I had to raise my eyes to locate the other two targets, one of which was trying to get in a parked car. I shot him twice in the chest, choosing to kill him reliably, by not trying for the head shot. The fourth target was running through the now panicked crowd, his robes flowing in the breeze as he ran. I fired three times, almost indiscriminately, and at least two of the rounds connected. But I couldn't be certain at the time that he was dead.

Quickly I turned my attention to the still unconscious figure on the floor. He was Arab, almost certainly Saudi given the circumstances. I had no instructions for a situation like this one. The life of the man sprawled on the floor came down to whether I thought he could identify me. It may have been a mistake, but I was willing to gamble that he wouldn't have been able to. That it had happened too fast, and he had never seen me straight on. But looking back, now I think I just didn't want to kill him. I had survived my own lack of professionalism and, I thought, so should he. Besides, I wasn't ordered to kill him.

I left everything as it was and went straight down the stairs and into the street among the fleeing crowd. I forced myself to walk the exact same speed as the people around me and made my way to the SUV parked street side about half a mile away. My instructions had been to stay in New York City for the next couple of days unless things got hot.

I think it was fair to say that things had gotten hot. I jumped in the car, headed south, and just kept going.

TWELVE

I didn't do anything except drive south until I was almost out of gas somewhere in Maryland. I think that was where I took my first full breath and gave any thought at all to the events of a few hours ago. I don't know if it was fear, panic, resolve, or some odd combination of "feelings" that carried me south and out of immediate danger. But now it was time to get back to work.

Jane had not texted or called. I wasn't quite sure what to make of that. Maybe she thought I was dead. I certainly deserved to be. But I dutifully texted her while I was pumping gas, "3/4 for sure, sloppy." Seeing no immediate reply, I got back in the car and kept going. My "plan," if you could call it that, was to drive until midnight or so and take a room wherever I ended up. Probably North Carolina.

It was only then that I started to try to make some sense of the day's events. Who the fuck was that guy and how did he know I was there?

Killing those guys was a political act. Most likely a very complex and multilayered part of some strategy of Jane's that was bold and sophisticated. My own part in her plans was always blunt, straightforward. I can't even pretend to know what was going on. And I wasn't even sure I wanted to. Her overall goals were hers. And I already knew enough to know that she was, for lack of a better phrase, "one of the good guys." But that didn't mean I didn't need at least some explanation.

I found a decent place to stay, got myself fed, and settled in before calling Jane. For the first time she sounded happy to hear my voice when she asked, "Are you OK?"

By our standards, this was a moment of outrageous emotion. It was like watching Mr. Spock reading poetry and crying.

"I'm OK, AJ, but as you might expect I have a few questions. I don't expect you to answer everything, but I do need some answers. First, why did they all have to be done at once? You know better than anyone how hard that is. It almost feels like you wanted me to fail."

"You almost did," she interrupted, but I was undeterred.

"And while we're at it, who the fuck was that guy?"

Again she interrupted, "What guy? What are you talking about?"

This made me pause for a moment. Was she shitting me? She always seemed to know everything. Did she really not know that I almost got my head blown off?

"The Arab in the room, Jane." I continued, "He put a gun to the back of my head just as I was about to take the first shot. I had to fight for my life and still managed to take out your targets. By the way, did I get the fourth guy?"

My aunt seemed genuinely surprised. "Yes, John, you got him," she answered.

"So who the fuck was he?" I asked again. "Do you guys have a mole? How else would he know I was there?"

She thought for a moment before answering, "I can tell you for sure that we don't have a mole. There isn't even anyone who *could* be one. But the Saudis are legendary for paranoia, especially when they're overseas. It wouldn't surprise me if they were just combing the surrounding buildings and you got unlucky."

"No, AJ, I was lucky. I got away with being stupid, lazy, and careless. I didn't lock the door, and I didn't hear him come in. There's every good reason for me to be dead!"

She paused for a moment before answering, "I'm glad you said that, John, because if you didn't, I would have. So what did you do with the body?"

"What body?" I answered.

"The guy in the room, did you just leave the corpse and get out of there?"

Uh-oh, I thought to myself. I hadn't really considered what she might make of my decision to spare him. As Ricky Ricardo might say, "I had some 'splainin' to do!"

"Jane, he never saw me. I spun on him and took him down in like five seconds. I left him unconscious in the apartment."

The silence on the other end of the phone told me everything I needed to know. "Understand this, as if your life depends on it. Because it does. You will never leave anyone alive that may have had any chance of having seen you. This is not negotiable. I need to hear you answer yes before we can continue."

She was pissed and I didn't blame her. I already knew better.

"Yes," I said.

"Thank you," she replied simply. "But now I have another question. Where the fuck are you going?"

"Florida," I replied as if it was the only possible answer. "I'm on vacation, and that is not negotiable either. I'll have more questions about this mission, but they can wait. For now, I am on vacation."

She didn't argue the point. She just said, "I'll answer some of your questions and I'll help you to understand some of what has led up to what happened today. But you're right. it can wait."

I was going to answer her, but as was her custom, she'd already hung up.

Now it was time to contact Linda and throw myself on the sword.

"Florida?" I texted to her. Doing the best I could to distract her from my absences and less than normal behavior. "Mental patient?" was her reply. "Yes, but Florida?" The phone rang. "You disappear and then reappear for two days acting like you're on the spectrum and I'm just supposed to act like everything is fine?"

It occurred to me that at least two of the three women in my life had particularly abrupt telephone habits. I don't know. Maybe it's me. Perhaps I'm so exasperating that I rob people of their cordiality.

"Everything is fine now," I responded. "Please listen, honey. I had a couple of things that had to be worked out and it weighed heavy on me for a little while. But I am so sorry. The last thing I would ever want is to take any of that out on you. Was I really that bad?"

I could feel the now familiar playfulness return to her tone. "Look, John," she said. "I'm not trying to say I'm the hottest woman on the planet. But when I ask a man up to my apartment, the last thing I expect is some bitch-ass answer like, 'Oh, I don't feel good.' So what is this shit about Florida?"

"I'm in Florida," I said. And then amended it to say, "Well, actually, I'm on my way and I will be in Fort Lauderdale the day after tomorrow."

She replied quickly, "So I guess you just expect that I'm going to drop everything and meet you in Florida?"

"Well, yeah, that was kind of the idea. Not just that, I will even make the reservation and buy the flight."

There was no immediate reply, but I could almost hear her

wheels spinning. "OK, John, but I'm still not gonna fuck you, whether you buy the ticket or not. I might be for sale but not that cheap."

I smiled to myself and said, "I expect nothing from you but your delightful company," which I had meant to sound a little sarcastic, but it had somehow come out in complete earnest. "Also, you may have to put sunscreen on my balls once in a while. It's hard for me to reach and you have no idea how painful sunburned balls can be. Actually neither do I, now that I think about it."

I got my payoff. Her laughter really was music to my ears, and I knew I would see her again soon.

"OK, John. And just to show there are no hard feelings, I'll even tell you my last name and spare you the embarrassment of having to ask. Because I know you have no fucken clue. It's Davidson." And then she spelled it out for me like I was a two-year-old sniffing the crayons as I wrote.

I made the reservation for her on my phone the next time I stopped. I texted her the flight information, adding, "1-way ticket to nowhere . . . but at least you can leave when I get obnoxious."

"If that were the test, I wouldn't be coming in the first place," she answered, adding a little smiley emoji.

The next day was all driving. And not at all surprisingly, a phone call from Kate. No doubt to sniff out my state of mind.

"So, John, do you like you?" she asked, before even saying hello.

This, of course, was completely out of the blue and not at all what I was expecting. I started to wonder. I have three women in my life and all of them always seem to be at least three steps ahead of me at all times.

"I don't know, Kate," I answered, trying to buy some time to think about it. "We both know what I do, but all in all I would say I'm a pretty good guy. I don't go out of my way to be a dick and, like everyone else on the planet, I at least think I have a pretty good sense of humor."

She waited patiently until I paused before answering, "OK, great. For the record I happen to agree, and yes, you do have a decent sense of humor, and on top of that you aren't too hard to look at. So, do you like Linda?"

If anyone else had said something like that to me, I would start to think she was hitting on me. But I discarded that theory, thinking that of course Kate and Jane had to know that both Linda and I were on our way to meet up in Fort Lauderdale.

"Of course," I finally responded. "Why else would I send her a ticket to come meet me?"

"So why do you like her?" Kate asked innocently.

"Look, Kate," I responded, "I think I know where you're going with this. Of course I'm sexually attracted to her. I'm still a man after all. Aa weird one maybe, but still a man at the end of the day."

"That's nice to know, John, but not the point. You like Linda because you like you. And from everything you have told me about her she is a lot like you. How could you not like her, John? She's you but with tits."

I laughed out loud at this, but of course, her analysis was probably spot on.

"So let me get this straight. I am such a narcissist that I want to fuck myself?"

"I wouldn't put it exactly like that, but yes, you are attracted to a person who is like you. I wouldn't exactly call that narcissism, and even if it is, I suspect it's still a healthy one. You are completely allowed to like yourself and you are also allowed to like someone who is similar to you. There is nothing wrong with that."

As usual, I was given a shit ton to absorb in a very short conversation.

"So can I take this to mean that Linda and I have your blessing?" I asked in a tone as if I was asking a priest for forgiveness in the confessional.

"Sure, why not?" she said and laughed. "Enjoy yourself, John. Enjoy your vacation. It might be a while before you get another one."

Of course, she hung up before I could answer. It seems that in this life I will never get the last word. Though there are some folks back in New York who might beg to differ.

I booked my own apartment in Fort Lauderdale a block from the beach. I have no idea why I did that, because I hate the beach. I hate it so much that I have absolutely no idea why anybody likes it. There is exactly one good thing about the beach: women in bikinis. The rest is a wet, sandy, sunburned mess. I know I'm an outlier on this one. Most people seem to love it. I enjoy an ocean view as much as the next person. But laying down and baking in the sand has zero appeal to me. And going in the ocean has even less appeal, if that's possible. Seaweed, man-o-war, sharks, and god knows what other kind of shit is swirling around in there. And they are best left alone. That is their space. You don't see dolphins rolling up to Starbucks with their tablets looking for a latte. So, it's simple. I stay out of their space, and they stay out of mine. It's the same kind of arrangement I have with horses. I agree to not try to climb on their backs and they agree not to throw me off and kick me in the face. It works out well for everyone.

The apartment was nice, about a block off the beach. It felt very private, even though it really wasn't. It was exactly as it looked in the pictures online. Clean and with a gray and black color scheme throughout. I had booked it for a month and hoped very much that I would get to stay—that *we* would get to stay that long.

I picked Linda up at the airport. I brought nothing with me other than a little bit of cash. The reason being that AJ had an aversion when it came to me and airports. In Jane's mind, airports would always be inordinately dangerous for me. Even if I wasn't flying. I thought it was something close to paranoia on her part.

Nevertheless, I obeyed her wishes and drove completely clean to pick up Linda. I was pleasantly surprised to see that Linda was traveling light, pulling only a medium-sized rolling duffel behind her.

I jumped out of the car and hugged her, and she hugged back. I don't know the science, but it has to be something chemical. My brain was flooded with endorphins at the sight of her. It was a quick embrace in a crowded airport pickup lane, so we both jumped quickly back in the car.

"I can't believe I did this," she said out loud to no one in particular. "Have you ever been here before?" I asked, adding, "It's my first time here."

"Yeah," she answered. "I was here with my parents, but I was real little. I don't remember it much."

"Well, it's kind of like New York, but warmer and different bugs."

She seemed to like the apartment and stepped out onto the balcony, saying, "So that's what an ocean looks like. It's been a while. By the way, one bedroom? Were you planning on sleeping on the couch, cause I'm sure not."

I'd crept up behind her as she spoke and wrapped my arms around her waist. I said, "No, I was planning on lying next to you in the bed, but not on you, unless you ask very, very nicely."

I quieted her ensuing laughter with a soft kiss, a kiss that she didn't resist.

THIRTEEN

We quickly fell into something of a rhythm. Linda, as it so happens, loves the beach but didn't try to force me down there other than for an occasional walk along the shore at sunset. Which even I had to admit was pretty nice. She was in the habit of going early in the morning, more often than not before I would even wake up. I was never much of an early riser and neither is she. But she would head for the beach almost every day at about 10. Usually she would return before she might get extra crispy around 1 p.m. I loved having her with me. But I think we both also loved the alone time we would get each day. As Kate had said, we really were alike in a lot of ways.

It shocked me how quickly I got used to sleeping next to her. I had never really slept next to anyone. The girlfriends of my teens and twenties had all returned to their own homes. This was completely new to me, and I already knew that it would feel weird to sleep alone when that time came again, which it had to sooner or later. There was still no sex, but I never pushed. She knows I want it and I know I want it. And if she really doesn't want to have sex, then she is putting on a hell of an act. I am far from an expert, but I'm pretty certain sure she'd had plenty of orgasms when we would "play." Which is what she would call it when she was feeling frisky.

There didn't seem to be much of a problem about her missing work or school. She told me the coffee shop had made her quit when she left for an indefinite time. But they had also promised to immediately rehire her upon her return. As for school, I would see her do some work on the laptop she had brought along. Occasionally she would be on the phone with one of her professors. On my end, there was an occasional text from Jane or Kate but no pressure to get back to work. No mission orders.

Three weeks went by before I got a serious call from Jane. It came right after Linda had left for the beach, so we would definitely have some uninterrupted time to speak. The problem was that there was some asshole on the beach driving an incredibly loud ATV. I found out later that they were not legal on Fort Lauderdale Beach. But apparently nobody enforced it. Well, nobody except me, that is. I was easily a hundred yards from the beach with a closed balcony door and I still couldn't hear a damn thing every time this douchebag went by. I could only imagine how obnoxious it must have been to the people actually on the beach. This guy had been there almost every day since I had arrived. He'd woken me up more times than I could count. Enough was enough.

I was on the phone with Jane and I think that she was telling me that I might have to go to France soon for a mission. But honestly, I wasn't sure because every thirty seconds or so this guy would go by and I couldn't hear a damn thing. I'd made up my mind. As the conversation continued on and off, I pulled the three sections of my gun from where I had hidden it and grabbed a box of shells. I assembled and loaded the weapon as I cradled the phone by my ear with my shoulder. When it was fully assembled and ready, I asked Jane to hold on.

This was not a difficult shot. Especially compared to my recent work. The only complication was that the beach was crowded. I had to make sure that the vehicle wouldn't plow into anyone once the rider had been dispatched. There was an incredible amount of noise coming from that vehicle. So much so that I wasn't so worried about any sound my weapon might make when discharged. He wasn't wearing a helmet, but I still chose a shot to the chest. He died instantly, as did the noise.

There must have been at least a thousand people within earshot of the now quiet bike. A roar of laughter and applause erupted across this section of Fort Lauderdale Beach. I almost felt as if I should take a bow. But instead, I returned to the phone where Jane still waited for me. The crowd celebrated for a full thirty seconds before a few people approached the wreck and realized that the former rider was dead. But it took a little while for the news to spread. Like a wave rippling through the crowd below. The mood changed from one of joy to one of shock. But there was no stampede. No one had heard a shot. No one felt threatened or afraid. It's as if a single lightning bolt had descended from the sky and then vanished as quickly as it had come.

Meanwhile I resumed the conversation with Jane, disassembling the weapon as we spoke. I returned it safely to its hiding spot. It was not a sophisticated location. I would never try to go through an airport with it. It was just the zippered bottom of a rolling suitcase that opens separately. Probably meant to keep shoes or soiled clothing separate from the rest of your stuff. The zipper is visible from the outside, but I was never worried that Linda might find it. Maybe I should've been, but I would never consider searching her luggage, so I couldn't imagine she would search mine.

Jane was telling me that vacation time was coming to a close and that there were several possible missions on the horizon. Including the possibility of a trip to France. The police had come. I had noticed that they are never far away on the ocean front. The ambulance had come and taken the dead douchebag away. A flatbed truck removed the wreckage. Less than an hour later it was as if it had never happened.

That's when the phone rang again.

"What the fuck did you do?" It was Jane again. "Did you just pop some moron on the beach?" she asked.

"Yeah," I answered. "He was so loud I couldn't hear a goddamn thing you were saying when you were trying to talk to me. Seriously, this guy has been terrorizing this section of beach the whole time I've been here. Trust me, there's not a lot of gray area here. This jerkoff had it coming."

It took a few seconds for her to reply, "I don't give a shit about why you did it. In fact, I don't doubt for a second that this idiot had it coming, but now you are famous, you putz!"

"What are you talking about?" I asked, confused. "It was less than an hour ago."

I should have realized what was coming next.

"Social media, genius. God knows how many people filmed it, and now it's trending on every platform. Nice shot, by the way, but it's already been viewed almost half a million times. Just because you're not into social media doesn't mean the rest of the world isn't. You're famous now! Well, not you, per se, thank god. They've even come up with a nickname for you already. IIts flooding the comments. Congratulations, asshole, you're The Silencer."

I was in shock. And she was, as usual, completely right. I didn't even think about social media. But a quick look on my own confirmed that a fuck ton of people are into it. Already, just while we were talking, the number of views was reaching a million. People on social media rarely agree about anything. But everyone seemed to agree that I was The Silencer. There were videos from a few different angles floating around, but they were more or less the same. The roar of the ATV going by, no sound of a shot, but a very sudden and final silence as the vehicle rolled over and came to a stop in the sand. None of the videos really captured what happened to the rider, but the comments reflected that everyone knew he had been shot. Surprisingly, no video of the bloody corpse ever surfaced.

I felt not the slightest shred of guilt, nor any regret for having done it. Maybe this guy didn't wake up today, look in the mirror, and say to himself, "Good morning, asshole. Today we're going out to annoy as many people as possible." But the fact is that he did. He desperately wanted attention. It was unfortunate for him that he gained mine.

It occurred to me that there may be a benefit to the fame this incident had already generated. Someone might now think twice before setting out to be a jerk. This would be a good thing. A very good thing.

Jane was still on the phone, and I asked her if she thought I was in any danger of being exposed and should I get Linda and myself out of here.

"Nah," she responded convincingly. "Cops aren't like you see on TV. It's always some hot girl who also happens to be a detective and a genius at forensics. It doesn't work that way in real life. They will look into it because it's high profile, but I can't imagine they can put it together. You are as safe there as anywhere. But you can't stay forever, John. The world's problems didn't go away just because you got spooked and needed a vacation. And I can't imagine that Linda can stay away forever either. She must have some sort of life to get back to." Of course, she was right.

"Probably," I agreed. "But it's not fair, I should have gotten to pick my own nickname if I was going to get one."

She laughed, which is something AJ doesn't do a whole lot of. "You should really be called The Putz. Just be happy with what you got because it's actually kind of cool. Besides, you are my first employee to become famous. We just better hope nobody ever finds out who you actually are. I probably shouldn't have to remind you that being famous is not a good thing in this business."

I was only half listening and responded with, "I would've preferred Dick Slayer or maybe The Muter."

She ignored me. "Goodbye, John," she said before adding, "You will receive new mission orders next week." She hung up.

Well, at least she said goodbye for once.

It was still another hour before Linda got back from the beach. It had not occurred to me until after the fact that she might be nearby. Or that she could conceivably have been a witness. She wasn't. She was actually a few hundred yards down the beach. She had heard the ATV like everyone else and also noticed it had gone silent. It wasn't until she was walking back to the apartment that she heard about the incident. And then found it on social media.

"Holy shit, John!" she was telling me excitedly. "Some asshole got shot down on the beach."

I feigned curiosity, saying, "I heard, but why would you say he was an asshole?"

"Because it was that dick who rode that crazy loud bike every day. You've heard it. You complain about it every time you hear it."

"Oh, that guy!" I said, sounding surprised. "Well, I hate to see anyone get hurt, but if someone had to go it might as well have been him."

She looked up at me but didn't say anything. I got the sense that she felt the same way but thought it might be wrong to admit it out loud.

"Well at least we don't have to hear that shit anymore," I said with a smile. I decided that it was the right time to bring up that our almost month-long play date was going to end soon.

"I really am sorry about what happened today," I lied. "It's crazy that something like that could happen with so many people around." I added, "Baby, we have to leave soon, maybe another week or so, but then we have to get back to the real world."

She didn't complain, but she did kind of chuckle and say, "Real world? What do you know about the real world? The real world is that nasty coffee shop and a shitload of homework that I let slide. But you're right, it is about that time. Fly me home on Sunday." That was six days away.

"I can hit the coffee shop and track down some of my professors next Monday morning, start trying to get caught up."

I nodded, looking into those eyes that still got to me every time I saw them.

"It's been fun, hasn't it?" I said a little wistfully.

"It's not quite over yet," she replied and smiled a little naughty kind of smile.

I think we both understood what she was referring to. She had been standing in the kitchen, her back pressed against the counter. I picked her up with a swiftness and ease that surprised her and carried her caveman style over my shoulder to the bedroom. Putting her down gently on the bed, I "laid all over her" for the better part of an hour. But the rules of the game had not yet changed. And by now I had figured out the rules. She gets to come. I get to watch.

That week went by absurdly fast. I had received part of my mission orders. I would start driving to Houston next Wednesday. I was still driving around in the SUV with New York plates. Jane told me that she would wait until after Linda left and then switch out that car for one with Texas plates registered to me. I would not be traveling with any weapons. This was just part of her kind of caution. There was just no reason to have me driving around with a weapon that could raise questions, should I get caught up in a traffic stop. Or that might be illegal depending on where I was.

And Jane had told me a while back that she wanted me flying as little as possible. All kinds of bad things can happen at airports. Not the least of which were the identification requirements, records, and cameras. I was actually a little sad to have to part with my weapon. I wasn't usually sentimental when it came to hardware, but this one had become my favorite. So much so that I had given it a name, though not a particularly clever one. It was a Barrett M82, so it had become Barry. I sadly but dutifully disassembled Barry into a dozen pieces and disposed of him in a dozen different trash cans throughout the city.

I'd be lying if I said that I wasn't hoping for some kind of final "consummation" of my physical relationship with Linda before she had to leave. Our last day together was a lot like the rest. She went to the beach. I went for a light run, not on the beach. We had a nice dinner together at a restaurant that was part of a pier that extended over the ocean in an adjacent town called Dania Beach. It was actually quite romantic as we sat outside in the cool ocean breezes. By now I had acquired a little bit of a taste for wine. But of course, I was still clueless as to what might make one wine good and another bad. I just know what tastes good. That night quite a bit of it tasted good to both of us. We had walked the mile or so from our apartment to the pier. Two hours later we wandered back in no particular hurry.

When we got home, a tired Linda headed straight for the bedroom, shedding her clothes and shoes as she went. I did the same, and moments later it was her and me in our bed. Me in my underwear, she in her bra and panties. But I saw that what she was wearing was not her ordinary underclothes, which I had seen many times. They could better be described as lingerie. Needless to say, it had the desired effect and more.

Looking up at me she said, "I think I love you, John."

And before I could reply, she added, "Not to ruin the mood

or anything, but that was the first time I ever said that to anyone, and I'm not really sure what it means."

"It means something to me," I said, kissing her rather passionately.

She returned the kiss, and it went on for longer than ever before. We were holding onto each other like two people who knew that they would soon be missing each other. Because that's exactly what we were. This was not the first time, but she soon shimmied down her panties and said, "Taste me, John." It was more like an order. One that I was more than happy to follow.

What happened next had not happened before as she reached back and started pulling on my own underwear, trying to pull them down. Again, I was more than happy to help and, moments later, my underwear was gone, as was her bra. We both got on our knees, fully naked together for the first time and facing each other.

It was Linda who pulled me to her, kissing me and pulling my hand to her breast. I could see that she was soaking wet. Part of me was waiting for the floor to fall out, that she would bring me very close but not quite to the goal. But that didn't happen. She quickly laid back, pulling me on top of her. Moments later she reached down and just pulled me right to her door. The feeling was indescribable as I was perched atop her, motionless and staring into her beautiful eyes. Those eyes told me all I needed to know, and a moment later I was inside her. I stayed motionless, fully inside, knowing that if I wasn't careful, all of these months of waiting would make for a very quick finale. So I began a very slow and steady pace. Linda didn't seem to mind. Her head went back and she wrapped her legs around me, crossed at the small of my back.

We stayed in this slow steady rhythm for five minutes or more, and I was already quite proud of myself. It may not seem like much, but with a woman like her below me and the seemingly endless months of waiting now behind us, it seemed at the time to be an epic accomplishment. She put her hands to my shoulders and began to wriggle out from under me. Then she was perched on her hands and knees and moved her body to the edge of the bed. I understood immediately what she wanted. I was to stand at the edge of the bed and enter her from behind. I didn't need to be told twice. It was a different but somehow even more intense experience. Even though I could no longer see her face, this still felt somehow more intimate. As if she was finally giving herself to me completely. Later she would tell me that the point of that was not the intimacy. It was simply that she knew it would make us both come incredibly hard. And as is almost always the case with the women of my life, she was right. It was almost five minutes before I exploded inside her. And if I read the room correctly, she was right there with me, coming hard and loud. We both collapsed in a sweaty heap on the bed.

There was more. A lot more. At least six more positions, a few I had never seen before. Every burst of sexual passion was followed by a rest period.

She looked at the clock and realized it was 4 a.m. We had been at this for more than four hours. Her flight was at 7. "Jesus Christ, John. Do you ever let me get any sleep? I'm gonna be a zombie on the plane. Let's take a shower."

Three hours and a few cups of coffee later she was gone. I was going to miss her horribly, a longing I had never known before. And I was certain she felt the same way. But this woman was so worth waiting for. Every single minute, every moment of frustration had been worth it. And more.

FOURTEEN

I had received the remainder of my mission orders and was on my way to Houston. As usual, I had some questions, but I was sure that I would be speaking with Jane and probably Kate along the way. That seemed to be our pattern. My primary target was a very well-known pastor of a super church, Jimmy Grahm. Even I had heard of him. He was one of the newish brands of "Prosperity Preachers." The idea being that if you believe in Jesus enough and sent money to the pastor, you will be rich and good looking. Most of the people I saw in his TV broadcasts would still be fucken ugly even if they gave the preacher every penny and lost the hundred extra pounds they were carrying around. It would be an unusual mission for me, to say the least. The guy was very well protected. Plenty of guards and he seemed to know somehow to avoid city blocks with tall adjacent buildings, which was pretty much my forte. His only weakness was that he had an irrational desire to drive himself wherever he went. Yes, he had guards on board so you still couldn't just walk up and pop him, but this desire to be the driver would soon be the death of him if I had anything to say about it.

There were also another handful of drug guys. It seemed that this fentanyl thing was spreading and Jane once again wanted me to clean house. Now in the Houston market. Jane seemed to want to keep driving home the point that if you want to keep adding fentanyl to street drugs it might very well be you that ends up dead. The group in Houston apparently hadn't gotten the message yet. For the first time, one of my soon-to-be victims was black. Don't ask me why, but on some level I had a problem with that. But I am also aware that it makes no sense. If he is what Jane makes him out to be, he more than has it coming. But for some reason I just did not want to shoot a black guy.

Perhaps I just felt as if they had enough problems just by being black. My victim was the result of hundreds of years of dehumanization and abuse. But at the end of the day there are plenty of black people who have endured all of that and don't do harm to people and the community. I would do my job. But that didn't mean I'd be happy about it.

Grahm would be first. And for the first time I would be using my recently acquired and still quite rudimentary surveillance skills. I was to watch him for a few days. Try to find a weak spot and get the job done. It's the most autonomy I'd been given so far, not counting Florida, of course. After that, assuming there was no heat, I would spend as much time as I needed to dispatch the drug dealers. There was a pattern. There was the main target and then, as long as I was there, why not pop the local bad guys?

A couple of hours into my drive I got the phone call from Jane. I was ready.

"So you want me to pop a Rabbi?" I asked, knowing full well he wasn't.

"No, schmuck, he's a billionaire pastor followed by millions. Trouble is he makes most of his millions by money laundering for Mexican cartels and the rest of it by fleecing his poor rubes out of their hard-earned dough. And if that wasn't enough, he's also protecting at least a dozen pedophiles among his associate pastors. This guy truly is the Swiss army knife of shitheads. And the drug dealers are the same deal as up north. The morons keep killing their customers. But we have other matters to discuss."

I was not surprised.

"Now that we have a little time. Let me tell you a little bit about the Saudis and how they fit into this overall puzzle. The first thing to know is that they really are the bad guys. Most of the time in our business we wander through a lot of gray areas. This isn't one of those times. The Saudis suck balls."

I got to use one of my favorite lines. "AJ, it's best if you try to open up. Don't sugarcoat it".

I barely got the last word out before she cut me off, "Shut up, John, this is the real stuff."

"The Saudis have been making billions a year from the sale of oil for more than a century. They've used a lot of that money to create, fund, and execute terror throughout the world. They even founded, fund, and operate Wahhabi schools that teach the most extreme form of Islam and are basically terrorist groomers. Other than oil, terrorism is their biggest export. Most of the Taliban went through that system as did most of the 9/11 terrorists. With their vast wealth and power, they have found willing accomplices in the United States. Including the Bush Family. Who have done their bidding for over a century."

I interrupted at this point, "AJ, I thought we were an apolitical kind of deal. All of this sounds pretty political."

"I'm glad you said that, John. There is a difference between politics and reality, but of course they're going to overlap, at least a little bit. What I'm telling you is absolute reality. If that should reflect badly on a nation, politician, or person then so be it. But you and I must deal in reality. As you know, lives are at stake, including our own."

I ignored her little dig and just let her keep rolling.

"The Saudis have played both ends against the middle for over a century. On the surface they pretend to be our ally, but they are anything but. Fifteen of the nineteen 9/11 terrorists were Saudi. Some of them were even Saudi-trained pilots. But did we go after the Saudis, the people who actually attacked us? No. Instead we destroyed the Saudis enemies in Iraq and Afghanistan, making them even more powerful. In reality, they have dominated the United States and used us when it suits their purpose, which is to keep the world forever addicted to the oil that is destroying the planet. And of course they have plenty of help. This is where the conversation we had about CRAP and other corporate excesses ties into what we're talking about now. The Saudis are always one of the largest contributors to CRAP. The multinational oil companies have used their power, arguably to the benefit of the Saudis, to fight and destroy any form of public transport in the U.S., and I remind you again, these are in no way American companies. They are owned and run by foreign investors, again, to their own benefit. They are at best ambivalent to and more often hostile to American interests. Remember what you were told about reverse capitalism, where the taxpayers pay the employees and they make the profit. The externalities of oil are even more comically horrible."

I took it as a sign of respect that she just assumed that I understood what the term "externalities" meant. It's an economics concept. I sell you a gun, you buy it. Done deal, right? No. Even though it is a legal, private transaction, it has effects, or "externalities," that affect everyone, even those who don't own or care about guns. We know that with guns, a certain number of people will die and robberies will happen. Courts, police, lawyers, and hospitals will be involved. All of which cost taxpayers money. And the manufacturers wield so much political power that it is impossible to pass a law in the

U.S. that might help taxpayers recoup any of those costs. So Ruger sells Jimmy Bob Ray Earl a gun. Ruger makes profit, Jimmy Bob Ray Earl feels slightly less dickless, and the rest of us get to pick up the tab.

Jane continued, "The climate is being destroyed, and there have been countless wars and deaths. The mostly foreign-owned oil conglomerates even get direct cash subsidies from taxpayers due to the hapless and hopelessly corrupt politicians that the companies own. Not to mention the grotesque profits they earn while paying almost no taxes to offer any kind of offset. Think about it, John, even the U.S. fucking Navy is an externality of oil. We spend a trillion taxpayer dollars a year on national defense. A huge percentage of that goes to protect the shipping lanes for Saudi oil and plastic crap from the Chinese. More of it goes to protect the Saudis and other ludicrous douchebags from brown people who might try to stop us from getting oil from the Arabs or ninety-nine cent spatulas from the Chinese. Again we socialize the costs on the backs of American taxpayers and the multinationals pocket the profits, all while paying almost nothing in taxes. Again, this is not capitalism in anything other than name."

I had listened carefully throughout, despite the fact that there wasn't a whole lot in there that I didn't already know.

"So what the fuck are we doing, Jane? If you know what the problem is, then why aren't we fixing it?" I asked.

"You have been, John, one incompetently performed mission at a time. These problems didn't happen overnight, and they won't be fixed overnight. And the Saudis aren't the only bad guys. If you want to live long enough to actually make a difference, then you need to do what I tell you when I tell you. I'm going to assume that you already know that."

Then she hung up.

"I do know that," I said to Kate moments later. "But I can't shake the feeling that we can and should do more."

I'd called Kate right after Jane had hung up on me.

"John, you are twenty-seven years old and, despite what Jane might tell you, you're actually pretty mature for your age. And so far, at least, you're pretty good at your job. But one of the attributes of youth is impatience. And in your line of work, that can become an extremely unfortunate thing."

It didn't take a genius to decipher her point. Rather two points. One was that running around trying to fix the world with only my sniper rifle would probably work out poorly for me. The other was more implied: Jane would tolerate only so much. She had been annoyed by my freelance, unpaid work on Fort Lauderdale Beach and the resulting social media firestorm. Too much of that and Jane would be the one who would see to it that things worked out poorly for me.

I spoke with Linda a couple of times throughout the day, but we still mostly text messaged. She had gotten home safely and was well on her way to catching up with both her school-work and her job. With the idyllic life of the last month, we were both just a little bit down about returning to the real world. Though neither of us would admit it to the other.

"We left on a really, really high note," Linda told me.

And I responded with a simple, "Yeah, we did."

I stopped for the night about halfway. Somewhere near Tallahassee, Florida. More of the same the next day. I didn't hear anything else from Kate. But more details and intel were coming through from Jane on a regular basis, the last of which was the apartment I was to stay at in a suburb of Houston.

FIFTEEN

Ah, Jimmy Grahm. Son of the equally famous but now deceased the Reverend Bobby Joe Grahm, who was known over his sixty-year career as the Preacher to Presidents. The dead Grahm was by all accounts a halfway decent, sincere carrier of the Good Lord's word. That, of course, never stopped him from taking people's money. But it had been a different time for Christian evangelism in America. It wouldn't do to have the humble pastor flying around in a private jet or wearing three-thousand-dollar eel skin boots. Now, however, the over-the-top lavish lifestyles were the whole point.

Grahm was indeed quite cautious and clearly got a lot of good security advice from people who knew what they were doing. And he obviously listened to most of it. It would be most unfortunate for him that there was one area he didn't. Apparently, according to his bio, he had been in a minor car accident as a ten-year-old. He had been a passenger in a car driven by an employee of his father. There was no mention of whether he had worn a seatbelt, but the accident had broken his right arm and knocked out four of his front teeth. He often mentioned the accident in his lengthy sermons. Apparently, the Good Lord had seen fit to spare him and taught him a hard-learned lesson.

"I was spared!" he would yell and gesture to his right arm, which had never healed quite right. It worked but always seemed to hang awkwardly from his shoulder.

"The Lord wanted me to learn!" he thundered. "And learn I did. Once I was of age, I would put my safety in the hands of no man. I put my safety *only* in the loving hands of Jesus."

Apparently by "Jesus," he meant himself. He would only ride in a car driven himself. And, you guessed it, he was the only one to pilot his own private jet. Which so far, he had crashed twice. The Good Lord had shielded him from injury in both crashes. Further proof of his status as the chosen one. The Lord was less kind to the two staff members dead from the first crash and the other who had been left paralyzed from the neck down in the second. Apparently, their prayers to Jesus had been left unanswered.

It was no problem following him around. Why, because there was any number of mental patients who were following him around at any given time. Hoping, I guess, that some of his grace would fly off him as he drove his Bentley down the highway with burly, armed security guards in both the passenger and back seats. Perhaps hundred-dollar bills might come flying out the windows.

At first, he really did appear to be untouchable. But I would never report that to Jane. I could already hear her answer: "Everyone, and I mean everyone, can be erased." I knew what she would say, and I had no need to hear it, so I just kept patiently following. There was no hurry.

For the first time, my cache of weapons included a couple of handguns. Of course, they had left me a new Barry and one other sniper rifle. There was the possibility that I just couldn't get to him from a distance and, for a time, even I thought that may be the case. But the answer came eventually, and it came with a piping hot dish of irony on the side. Seems that a hurricane had hit Houston a few years back. Millions had been without power and huge sections of Houston had been underwater and uninhabitable for days. Federal aid came, but there were close to a hundred thousand people without a place to stay. Somehow a couple thousand of these desperate and hungry folks had found their way out to the massive Grahm estate in the very exclusive suburb of Piney Point. At that time, his estate was unfenced but covered by hundreds of cameras for the always-security-conscious Grahm. But the cameras couldn't stop the afflicted from seeking Grahm's blessing and perhaps a hot meal. They sat on the lush lawns and prayed. Grahm, of course, was not even there. Stupid, he wasn't, and he'd wanted no part of a Category Five hurricane.

It turned into a PR nightmare for the preacher, as he ordered all of the grubby, temporarily homeless people off of his lawn as the TV cameras were rolling. Of course he didn't personally kick them out. He got the cops to do it. He eventually blamed it all on the misunderstanding of an underling who he soon fired for so blatantly ignoring the sweet word of Jesus that demanded that we care for the needy.

But his reputation took a hit, temporarily at least. Never one to repeat a mistake, a massive fence was erected around the property a couple of months after the publicity died down. Never again would he risk bad publicity for kicking those damn kids off his lawn.

Normally the gate he would pass through would open without a hitch. This was top-of-the-line stuff. The rolling gates were the size of the driveway, which was about the width of a regular two-lane road. It was so precise that it would open only the one side he needed as he approached. There was a sensor on his vehicle that would alert the gate to roll open when he was about a hundred yards away. Nine times out of ten it would open and close perfectly. I know that because I had been watching every single day. The one day it started to open but stopped about halfway and not enough for the car to get through. I was thinking someone might get out of the car, but the gate resumed opening within ten seconds or so. This was my chance. It might take a while, but finally there was a slight chink in his armor.

First things first. I needed to know about the car. Initially I didn't like what I found out. It was an Armored Bentley Flying Spur. Rather than try to do the research myself, I passed all of the information along to Jane. With her resources I knew she could find out what, if anything, could pierce the windows of that car. I doubted that the weapon I had with me would accomplish the task. I wasn't even sure if anything would. There would be more to do. I would still need to find a position to shoot from. But there was no sense in doing that until I knew if I could shoot through the window of the Bentley.

The answer came two days later when a woman appeared at the door of my apartment. She wore no uniform. She was not military and not a delivery service. She simply handed me the box and left immediately.

I opened the box to find a weapon and ammunition I had never seen before. It had no markings or brand insignia. The box was otherwise empty save a short note written in pencil: *This will have a little more kick than you're used to, but no noisier. Love, AJ*

Now I could move on to the next set of problems. Grahm's house was in a very exclusive neighborhood, but the homes were not on massive lots. Don't get me wrong, they were big pieces of property compared to the rest of the world. But the biggest around was no more than an acre and a few were smaller. There were at least seven that would offer a usable sightline, and as many as five more, depending on the effective range of this weapon under the circumstances. In this case, closer really was better. I sent all this information to Jane, including photos of the neighborhood. I knew she had access to any information I might need about the homes and the possibility of using one. I wasn't interested in a suicide mission, and I was happy to hear Jane wasn't either. I wasn't going to just set up on someone's lawn and pop a famous pastor in broad daylight.

Fortunately, my aunt had created a quite elegant solution. She had found that one of the homes was unoccupied and for sale. In a neighborhood like this, there were no "for sale" signs and no open houses. She would send out a team to make the house safe for me to work from. That meant a lot of things. Any security system would have to be disabled. She would have to know if there were any showings scheduled. And probably at least a dozen other things I was nowhere near smart enough or experienced enough to have even thought of. Thinking about it now, the whole thing was still ridiculously dangerous. She must have really wanted this guy.

Eventually a plan was worked out. I had been surveilling him while waiting for Jane to do her magic, which took about a week. The good news now was that his gate had been getting worse. It was hesitating or stopping on an almost daily basis. I alerted Jane because any day he could have someone out to fix the problem. Had he done so, it would have made the mission all but impossible. This special weapon could pierce the windows, but almost certainly not if the car was moving. I needed it at a stop. If only for a few seconds.

Jane had made every arrangement. I pulled up to the house in a white van with the name Elmo's Plumbing and Supplies. I carried the assembled and loaded weapon in a large satchel slung over my shoulder that, on close inspection, would never have fooled anyone. Lucky for me no one was ever close enough. I sauntered through the unlocked door dressed in my white Elmo's Plumbing overalls. On the first day, the gate opened without a hitch and I dared not risk the shot as the Bentley moved smoothly through the gate.

On the second day, fortune smiled upon me. I could see through the scope that the gate had not fully opened. Peripherally I could see the brake lights on the Bentley light up.

I found my target and fired. A neck shot clean and perfect. She had not been joking. The kickback from the weapon nearly pushed me over. The window of the Bentley had not shattered. From where I was I couldn't even see the hole in the window. But I could see the body of Reverend Jimmy Grahm slumped over the steering wheel. Dead.

The irony was that the fences he built to keep out the needy turned out to be his death sentence. What better end for a greedy, thieving fraud. The thought pleased me and made me proud to have been the instrument of his destruction.

I walked calmly back to the van and drove to the destination predetermined by Jane where my car waited. It was near a warehouse just a few miles away. I somehow stripped off the overalls as I drove. I left the weapon and the overalls in the van, got in my car and drove off. I had just killed a famous man in front of his home in broad daylight.

Presumably Jane had somebody very nearby to immediately take care of the van and murder weapon, but I gave that no thought. It was done, and I told Jane so with the customary text, "Done," and followed it up for the first time with, "Now what?" I had been pre-instructed to just return to my apartment and await further instructions. Nothing had happened that would change that, but it still felt like the appropriate time for the "Now what?"

There had to be heat. The question would be how much. Could I stay and pursue my remaining assignments or was it time to get the fuck out of dodge? Only time and Jane would tell.

It didn't take long. I was barely through the door of my apartment when the phone rang.

"You might as well just get out of there, John," Jane said as if she were continuing a conversation that had already started. As usual she also anticipated what would have been my next question. "There's no particular threat or problem, but this is going to be a big deal. There's no sense in keeping you around there where a stray eye or camera could get you made."

By the time she'd finished the sentence, I was already throwing my few belongings into my suitcase. I walked into the bathroom to retrieve my toiletries and look around to make sure I didn't forget anything.

"Am I traveling light?" I asked, though I was already pretty certain of the answer.

"Yes," answered Jane. "I've already got cleaners nearby. Just start heading north."

That meant to once again leave the weapons behind and travel clean.

"Jane, if I go north I'll end up in North Dakota. You're gonna have to be just a bit more specific."

There was just a hint of impatience in her voice and she said, "Head back toward the Capital District. It could change, but just head that way. It'll take you three or four days anyway." Then she hung up.

I never took that personally. The constant hanging up and the way she would hit the ground running anytime we spoke. It was just her way. She was my boss, but she was still the same aunt that I remember from my childhood. There was just no bullshit in her game. But back to the Capital District? What, to pop more drug dealers? It's a big shitty world. There must be something more important for me to do than that. In my mind, I could do the world at least as much good by just going around popping people like Bob, or that guy on the beach in Fort Lauderdale. And I wouldn't even have to keep driving back and forth across the country to do it. I had just popped a particularly shitty, particularly famous person. I would do as I was told, but at that moment, I certainly didn't have to like it.

This was about as grouchy as I am capable of getting. So, naturally, the phone rang less than half an hour after I made it to the highway. It was Kate, of course. The women of my life know me better than I know myself. That is the only explanation I have.

"You're proud of yourself, aren't you?" I didn't immediately reply, and she continued with, "And why not? You saved the beach, did your job in Texas, and as far as I can tell, you got the girl."

That was about as specific as she could get on what we always regard as an unsecured line. And she was right. She always seemed to know exactly where I was mentally and emotionally. I was indeed feeling prideful. I am a sociopath, that is undeniable. But that doesn't mean I have no emotions at all. I'm not Mr. Spock. But I process them differently. I've never been anything else, so I have no more basis for comparison than a "normal" person might have in trying to compare themselves with me. If forced to guess at the difference, I would say that I see my life like a movie or photograph. I'm not "in" it. But I am looking at it and I am often interested in what I see. And what I see can make me feel things in the way that a normal person might cry during a sad movie. I am not living my life so much as viewing it. Is that good? Who am I to say? But I suspect that it means for me, and others like me, the stakes just never seem that high.

"Yes," I admitted. "I feel pretty good about the things I have done, and very, very good about Linda."

"That's OK, John," she said. "And you have every reason to be proud of yourself. But remember that pride is a double-edged sword. You absolutely must have confidence in order to be, well, you. But in your line of work, it's probably worse to have too much confidence than it would be to have too little. I'm not sure that made sense."

I interrupted her, "Yes, actually it makes perfect sense, I would like to think I learned a little something back in New York." Of course I was talking about the not dead Arab.

"OK," she said. "Now about Linda. Do you ever worry that your work might interfere with your relationship?"

"Well, inasmuch as if I had my way, she would be sitting next to me right now and sleeping next to me when I close my eyes tonight. But I suspect that everyone has obligations. I'm no different than anyone else."

She instantly replied with, "Well, that makes sense. Have you given any thought to what Jane was telling you about?

I had to think for a moment. Jane had told me so many things. But before Kate could interject it came to me.

"Heaven on earth?" I asked.

"Yes," she replied. "Well not exactly heaven on earth, but a planet where every child is assured of their most basic needs being met throughout their lives. The implications of that would be so massive that I don't think I have even fully grasped the concept yet, so I don't expect you have either."

"Well, Kate, it's not exactly like I've had a whole lot of time to think about it. I've spent more than a month chasing a Rabbi around."

She chuckled slightly and added, "Make the time, John. I don't know that there is anything more important, and it will add meaning to your work and your life, even if it doesn't feel that way in the moment. And don't get discouraged. Not everything you do will be world changing. And just in case you need reminding, it's quite possible that your actions saved the lives of virtually every person of color on the planet. I remember something that one of my professors said to me and it changed the way I looked at my job, and really the whole world: 'There are no big changes without many small changes.' I know it's not dramatic, but it helped me to understand that no good act is ever wasted or worthless. Every single step in the right direction is double, because it is also a step away from wrong."

I didn't respond right away because I really was listening to what she was saying. And damn if she hadn't once again given me the words I needed to hear when I needed them. The only response I could think of was, "Thank you, Kate. That really does help."

"I hope so, John. We'll talk again soon."

SIXTEEN

Ok, so it was back to the Capital District to pop a new group of emerging drug kingpins. I'm guessing that they'd regrouped faster than Jane had expected and that this new batch wasn't any smarter than the dead ones. They must still be lacing their products with fentanyl. These were suppositions but pretty basic and obvious ones. It was soon confirmed by the intel that was dribbling in from Jane while I was on the road.

As I drove, a thought occurred to me. If I were to simply keep popping every new drug-dealing leader that emerged, eventually someone would learn something. Not so grandiose as to think that it would completely stop the drug flow to these towns. Something more basic. They would have to adapt. And eventually they would have to figure out that lacing drugs with a deadly substance wasn't worth the price of being killed. By repeatedly chopping off the heads, we would eventually alter the behavior of the rest of the animals.

Why not apply that logic to bigger issues and problems? For arguments sake, let's say I went around popping the CEOs at every HMO in the U.S. They make decisions to benefit their shareholders at the expense of their customers' health. They do that every single day. It is their job to collect as many premiums as they can and deliver as little actual healthcare as humanly possible. It's what an economist would call "perverse incentives." The best interests of the company are always in direct conflict with the best interest of their customers, or victims. So you have referrals, wait times, ever increasing co-payments and outright refusals to cover certain conditions and medications. And a time-consuming and frustrating system of mediation on issues of coverage. These things are not accidental or incidental. It has been repeatedly revealed as true and intentional in court documents that these obstacles exist to enhance the bottom line. Even to the point that a "covered" customer becomes a liability when they receive a diagnosis that is sure to be costly to the company. It is very much in the best interest of the company if that person dies rather than receive numerous costly medicines and procedures. And they produce that result and reduce their financial exposure by subjecting the sick customer to any number of complicated and confusing obstacles. If this sounds horrible, you would be right. It is horrible. Evil is not a word I use lightly, especially given how I earn my daily bread, but in this case, it is the only word that will do. But it is business as usual for every HMO in existence. As Jane might say, "We must deal in reality. However awful that reality might be and however ugly it might make people look."

Is it possible we might coerce them into changing their behavior even though it means acting against the best interests of their shareholders, and for the best interest of their patients? Honestly, I don't know. But I would be more than game to find out.

In the back of my mind was the thought that I was being manipulated. That Jane and Kate were not so slowly planting notions such as these in my head. The bottom line is that, even if this were true, reality is still reality. Being steered into seeing the world for what it is doesn't bother me, nor does it alter that reality.

The next day I got some amazing news from Jane. I could stop in New York City and spend three days with Linda if I wanted to. She didn't need to tell me twice. There were strings attached, of course. Three more Saudis were to be dispatched. I would have my three days with Linda, then I would have to tell her I was leaving town but stay for as long as necessary to take care of the targets. Unlike last time, they would not all be in the same place at the same time and would probably require several different apartments to work from. Presumably Jane was working out the details.

"By the way," Jane said. "I know you don't look at this stuff, but it's my job to. The legend of The Silencer is growing online. Internet sleuths are connecting you to every shooting since Oswald."

"Seriously?" I asked. Even though there was no good reason for me to be surprised.

"Oh yeah," she continued. "There are dozens of threads on every social media platform that try to connect you to every-thing, even a few you actually did. There are whole groups devoted to you. Some of them are sharing sketches of what they think you look like. You might want to check it out. Some of the portraits are quite flattering."

"I'll pass on that, thanks," I answered. "But is this a prob-lem? Anything we should be worried about?"

Jane was reassuring in her own way. "I seriously doubt it, John. Unless you fuck up, The Silencer will remain just one of a million online conspiracy theories."

The first thing I did was call Linda. I was still a day and a half away from New York City and I was hoping she could free up some time for me while I was there. It occurred to me that we almost always text each other. And that most people now seem to text rather than call. Even before I started this life, I never listened to my voicemail. Anybody I knew and actually wanted to talk to would know just to text me. It's as if people have lost the ability to speak to each other, especially on the phone. It's almost an art form to know when there are natural pauses and breaks in a conversation and when it's time to speak and when it's time to listen. Now it seems that people just talk over each other. And even when they aren't speaking, they still aren't even listening. They're just waiting for their turn to speak. Maybe that's why people like texting so much. It's the only way we can express a full thought without being interrupted. It's a self-reinforcing phenomenon because the more we text, the less skilled we are at verbal interaction, and then again resort to texting. Have we lost something in this process? Maybe. I'll leave it to people smarter than me to sort it all out.

My own phone conversations are limited to three people: Kate, Linda, and Jane. Although I have spoken with my parents a couple of times. Not to pat myself on the back but I am an excellent listener, and that single skill has served me well. It all goes back to a teacher I had in grade school long ago. She said, "I've never learned a thing while I was talking." It stuck with me. It implies that the listener is almost always getting the better side of the bargain. With Jane I was always listening. My life depended on it. With Kate and Linda, it was closer to being an even exchange. Though with Linda there wasn't a whole lot I could say. "How was your day, honey?" I could imagine her asking me. To which I would reply, "Well, I shot three guys today before lunch. How was your day, sweetheart?"

Our actual conversation went a bit differently. She was thrilled that we would have some time together, and I was thrilled that she was thrilled. She had to work one of the days that I would be there, but other than that it was all clear. I invited her to stay with me in the apartment Jane had already arranged. She'd put me in Brooklyn for the recreational part of my stay. Actually, for the first four nights. After that would be a series of balcony apartments in and around the Turtle Bay area of Manhattan where my targets would be. None of which were anywhere near the coffee shop where Linda worked or the building I had stayed in during my first visit, the idea being to minimize the possibility of accidently bumping into Linda after I'd supposedly left. She rarely ever questioned me about where I was and what I was doing. And I, for my part, never questioned her. The subject had come up exactly once back in Fort Lauderdale. I told her one day that I was going for a run and that I would be back in an hour or two. And it was the truth. Her answer was, "Baby, you never owe me any explanations and I don't owe you any for that matter. I'm not going to fuck things up by needing to know what you're doing every minute. I trust you completely, unless you give me a reason not to." This was a long answer to a short question. It almost felt like she had been waiting for a reason to tell me that. After all, I was just going for a run.

"I've seen too many relationships ruined by stupid insecurity," she'd added.

I wrapped my arms around her waist and said, "I hope you know this without me needing to say it, but there is no one else in my life and I don't want there to be."

I saw her face light up and she said, "I feel the same way, baby, but if you cheat on me, I'll kill ya." There was just something about the way she smiled when she said it that made me think that maybe she wasn't entirely kidding. I would never give her a reason to find out.

Three days with Linda in New York City was like a pleasant blur that went by way too fast. I actually saw my first Broadway show. It was a musical and not exactly to my taste. But the time passed fairly quickly, which means it couldn't have been too bad. I would try it again if given the opportunity. Linda loved it and saved the Playbill, a little magazine they give you that tells you all about the cast and the production. At three hundred dollars for barely decent seats, they should most certainly give you something to remember it by. Linda kept the Playbills from every show she'd ever seen. She said she had about thirty and that she'd go more often if she could afford it. I made a mental note to myself that I would make it possible for her to see any show she wanted, whether I was in town or not. In a way it's how I knew that I really cared about her. I don't think I can experience love in the conventional sense. But I see myself finding gratification in her enjoying things. I didn't love the show, but she did. Watching her experiencing it was for me better than my own experience of it. I want to do more things like that. I want to take her on a roller coaster or to Disneyland. Any hokey shit that I think she might like. That voyeur-like second-person pleasure is new to me entirely. It's why I know that I care about her in a way I haven't experienced before and didn't even realize I was capable of.

That was also the first time I had spent any money on anything that could be considered nonessential. Not that Jane would ever give me a hard time about expenses, I just never really needed to buy anything. Presumably my "pay" was piling up in some offshore account. But I never gave it much thought. Money, it seems to me, only matters if you don't have any. My basic needs would always be guaranteed. The trick was to live long enough to spend it. But I remain acutely aware that almost no one else has that luxury.

How many people can really cough up two or three hundred dollars for a show ticket? Apparently plenty from the looks of things. Virtually every show on Broadway sells out almost every night. That's the odd duality of American life that is constantly confusing me. On one hand, I know from statistics and news reports that close to ninety percent of Americans are living paycheck to paycheck. Ninety percent are one illness, one car breakdown, or one firing away from complete desperation and the specter of homelessness. My life is no picnic. But I will never know the constant anxiety of financial struggle that is only getting worse with each day and each economic forecast. Jane's vision of a world without basic material need had never seemed further away. Was this ultimately our mission? Or was it just the musings of a powerful sociopath and her willing nephew? There was no doubt that Jane and Kate wanted me to at least think about it. They were something less than subtle and that was fine with me. If I was being led, there are certainly much worse things they could have in mind than world peace and prosperity. I was trying to peek through the keyhole and imagine what that world might look like. The times I would think about it led me to the conclusion that pretty much everything would be different. Virtually every action, every thought, and every relationship somehow leads back to our fear of being homeless and hungry. It's a question so basic and important that we don't even know how to ask it. What does a world without need even look like? Yet according to Jane, it was within our grasp if we wanted it.

Linda stayed with me all three nights. We parted early on the last morning. Linda dressed in her apron for her day at the coffee shop. I could offer her no firm idea on when we would see each other again, nor did she ask. We were mirages in each other's lives. A wonderful apparition that appears, delights, and then disappears again into the mist. It was probably not reasonable of me to think I should be her only one. She deserved someone who could fully devote themselves to her. There was no time I could even imagine that I could be that man. For the time being, she seemed satisfied with what I had to give. But I had no illusions that it could be maintained forever.

Now it was time for work. John the Saudi Slaughterer was back in business. Again, probably a more accurate name than The Silencer, but on the other hand, there were the cyclists in the city that were now silent. Maybe the name was more accurate than even the people who gave it to me knew.

I spent the next ten days hunting fairly elusive prey. I was once again using a Russian-made weapon. Sooner or later, I would need to ask why. But for now, I wasn't going to worry about it. I got the first one the first day with the first shot. It got trickier after that. Neither of the other two surfaced for three days. When one did, I had no decent sightline onto a very crowded street. I wouldn't risk hitting an innocent civilian. There was no reason to. No hurry to do anything other than wait until I could execute cleanly and properly.

I got the second target on a dark street at almost midnight. I got the sense that they knew they were in danger and were trying, unsuccessfully, to move with stealth and safety. With the second came a surprise. The man who had put the gun to my head was with him. That answered some questions. He was undoubtedly a bodyguard, probably in the employ of the Saudi government. Obviously not a very good bodyguard, seeing as I had popped everyone he guarded. I could easily have killed him as well before I left that apartment some months ago. I briefly wrestled with myself about reporting it to Jane, but not seriously. I had made this decision to play her game, so I would play by her rules. She was not at all surprised by this revelation and remarked that it was actually a good thing. If that guy had made me, we would have known it by now. I stayed in town even after I had dispatched the third and final target. My goal was to get a photograph of this hapless Saudi bodyguard. I passed it along to Jane so she could ID him, just in case. She had agreed that the photo was worth taking the time to get.

Now it was back upstate to pop the rising stars of the Capital District drug trade. By the time I got there, the list of targets was up to seven. While looking through the photographs of the soon-to-be doomed, it occurred to me that all of my victims so far had been male. These seven were no different. How would I handle it if the person on the other end of my weapon were a woman? It wouldn't be long before I found out. But for now, I had my plate full.

I got two of them together on the second day of the hunt. It was one of the easier assignments of mine so far. But then came a call from Jane. Intel was pouring into my phone as we spoke. Operations had cranked back up at the laboratory in Allset. Oddly enough, it was a Hindu woman who had picked up where the thoroughly despicable Forrest Reagan had left off. This was complicated shit and Jane was giving me way more information about the project than I was used to. I sensed for the first time that Jane herself was a bit rattled that this massive, existential threat had reemerged, and so quickly.

She had already known that the Indian government had been one of the entities that had provided startup money to Geneworks, the company developing the technology. Jane had not been sure whether the Indian government was aware of Geneworks' real mission though. Now it was certain that they knew. They were more involved than ever, including providing a new leader to the operation which was reorganizing as we spoke.

I was to stop what I was doing immediately and hightail it to Allset. My mission was to pop this woman that I had immediately began referring to as Dotty from the moment I saw her picture. She was an Indian woman of Hindu descent who wore the traditional bindi, the red dot on her forehead.

"Could you possibly be more juvenile?" asked Jane when I referred to our target in Allset as Dotty. I don't know why it amused me so much, but it did.

I rushed back to Allset to the same room in the same Native American casino as before. The same weapon awaited me, and all I needed to do was wait for her arrival the next morning. She wasn't quite so precise in her habits as Forrest had been, but it was a sure bet that she would be climbing those steps sometime between 7:30 and 9 a.m. I was ready.

At 8:03 the next morning, I popped my first woman, my first Indian national, and my first Hindu, all in one person. And yes, I shot straight through the dot. It's a good thing I did. According to Jane, these fuckers were getting really close. Another week or two and they would have had at their disposal at least one strain of virus with the ability to kill nearly every black person on earth.

On my drive back to the Capital District, I told Jane that if I ever had to come back to Allset, it would be with explosives to simply blow the place up. An empty brag, we both knew since I had not even a minute of training with explosives.

"You won't have to," she answered. "If it comes to that, I will find someone to blow the place up ourselves."

We ended up having one of the most candid conversations in our history. She told me that it took her a while to learn why the Indian government would involve themselves in this genocide. And the answer was just as disgusting. From everything Jane knew, the Government of India had figured that an African continent nearly void of human life would give them a huge opportunity to control much of the continent and its resources. Not to mention space to spread out their massive population. Logical, but disgusting, even by our standards. I took it as a sign of growth. That Jane was willing to share so much of the information and motivation with me. I doubt very seriously that this would have happened when we had begun together, now well over a year ago.

Again, I drove back to the Capital District to complete my assignments. There were still five to go. I couldn't shake the feeling that we weren't making any real progress. That, far from changing the world, I was more like a fireman rushing from place to place, putting out the flames threatening to envelope us.

"You, sir, are probably the most important civil rights activist in the history of the world," said Kate. She had called on my way back to the Capital District. As usual, she seemed to know my thoughts as, and sometimes before, I had them.

"Great," I answered sarcastically. "I am the Rosa Parks of snipers." Which I immediately realized was something I should not have said on a phone call with Kate. She made no mention of it though and continued.

"You act like that's nothing. I don't think you really understand what was going on there," she said. At least Kate was smart enough to know that she couldn't get too graphic on a line we couldn't assume was perfectly secure. "But you, yes, you, singlehandedly stopped what would have been the worst disaster in the history of the world."

"Yes, Kate, I understand that, and I have no doubt that there are parts of the world that are better now than they would have been without me. But when do we get to go on offense? When do we get to do anything other than put out fires?"

It was weird. In some ways I felt closer to Kate than I did to Jane, or even Linda in some ways. Had I not met Linda, I may very well have thought of Kate as a woman I could have a relationship with. Or at the very least cheap, raunchy sex, I playfully thought to myself. Kate was a beautiful woman in her own right. Perhaps a little too old for me, but I'm not completely sure about that. I hadn't seen her in person for a while, but we had a few video calls. I would say she was in her early thirties at the most. I had no idea if she had a boyfriend, husband, or kids. She never shared any personal information about herself. All I knew was that she was physically very attractive, worked for Jane, and was always there for me when I needed her. Sometimes even before I even knew I needed her. There have been full-blown relationships based on a lot less. For her part, I may have read the room wrong because understanding female behavior has never been my strong suit. But there had been times where I felt that she may very well have had an interest in me that went beyond her professional duties. I wasn't sure, and ultimately it didn't matter. It was nothing short of miraculous that I still had Linda, and that was more than enough for me. Plus, there was the fact that I could not imagine Jane approving of any such shenanigans between two of her employees.

It took me nearly two weeks to complete my assignments in the Capital District. There were no calls from Kate or Jane. Linda and I spoke or texted every day. She was excited that she was only a couple of weeks away from graduation. Soon she would have a hard-earned master's degree in psychology. Probably a must if she was to continue a relationship with me, I thought to myself.

I had sent my now traditional text to Jane: "Done." But there was no immediate reply or further instructions.

SEVENTEEN

John has exceeded all of my expectations—and they were pretty high expectations to begin with. It seems like forever ago that we sat in Chipotle musing over the merits of our company and passersby. But in reality, it was already more than eighteen months ago.

He had more or less avoided the pitfalls of the trade, including, thank god, the god complex that had inflicted almost all of my previous snipers at one time or another, though he had flirted it with it once or twice, according to Kate. But he had shown one trait the others had not: impatience. This boy, like me, wants to fix the world. Unlike me, he wants it done now. It doesn't work like that, I'm afraid. The best we can hope for is two steps forward followed by one step back.

There was a good reason for his returning to the Capital District, and it's still more than likely that he will be there again, mowing down yet another group of drug dealers, whether they have learned their lesson about the use of fentanyl or not. The true purpose of the return trips was more of a psychological experiment in behavior modification.

Can we change the behavior of a large organization if we're

continually chopping off the heads of its leadership? The result of these experiments can have profound implications for the rest of the world.

If we did indeed assassinate the CEOs of every HMO in the world, would it eventually change their behavior for the good of their customers? The truth is, I don't know yet. But just like John, I am game to find out. It would, in effect, be forcing massive corporate entities to act against their own financial best interest. I have my doubts that even hundreds of 'beheadings', for lack of a better word, would bring about enduring change.

If I killed every leader of any fast-food corporation over and over, would that ween them off the public tit? Would they then pay every employee a living wage so that their employees' survival did not depend on the largesse of the American taxpayer?

The average American taxpayer was not in much better shape themselves. The multinationals have become so expert at avoiding taxation almost everywhere they do business. So again, it is the American taxpayer footing the bill for all the critical infrastructure that makes doing any kind of business possible.

Capitalism in the twenty-first century has morphed into a form of socialism. Huge corporations, American only in name, have learned to avoid taxes to themselves, even passing much of their own costs to taxpayers. The result is a form of socialism where the costs of doing business are socialized by way of taxpayer dollars, while the profits they earn on the backs of those taxpayers are private. It is the exact opposite of capitalism.

Flipping through TV channels the other day, I found a rarity, a talking head on television that said something that made sense: "Capitalism and free markets are the greatest creators of widespread wealth in the history of the world. We should try it sometime." Exactly.

Knowing the problems is one thing. Fixing them is quite another. I am in a position to do things that no one else can. A responsibility I will never take lightly.

John is impatient. But now I am ready to indulge him. Together we will take the first step of a great experiment. His next target is the CEO of the nation's second-largest HMO, a man named Grant Pearson. Why not the largest HMO? Because this gentleman is on public record for having said the quiet parts out loud. Not that it was his choice. He was forced to testify in a wrongful death suit brought by the family of one of his deceased customers. In court testimony, he admitted that the dead woman might still be alive had his company not drastically slowed the pace of her care with what he called "unfortunate administrative roadblocks." The company went on to lose that case, and a jury had awarded the family a multimillion-dollar judgment. That was more than three years ago, and the family has still not seen a penny. There have since been three appeals of that decision and a fourth is now proceeding. This one will almost certainly result in a drastically reduced or eliminated award, as the case now sits in the courtroom of a judge handpicked by the company as one who sides almost always with businesses over individuals. And even if that were not the case, "justice delayed is justice denied," as the saying goes. If there is one thing that John and I can provide, it is prompt justice. This time I needed to make sure he was going alone. This assignment was too important to permit the possibility of any emotional distractions.

Kate has also performed her duties admirably. Although I have one point of concern. There are moments that her reports to me seem to reflect something more than professional approval of John and his performance. I am the last one to claim to be an expert on male-female romance or relationships, but I'm beginning to sense that her interest in John might be moving beyond the professional. It would not be the first time that an assigned therapist had crossed this line. And the problem could be easily solved. I would simply assign him someone else. For now, I don't believe that is necessary, but I will continue to monitor the situation.

I think John will be quite happy with his next assignment. Any lingering doubts he had of just running in circles putting out fires should be put to rest. At least for a while anyway. It is easy to forget sometimes. But he is still a child, and children have very short memories.

EIGHTEEN

To say I was thrilled with my next assignment was one of the world's great understatements. I was born into a military family and have been spared the price of private healthcare in America. The price of time, money, humiliation, and death. But I had studied this inexplicably horrible system extensively. And as bad as you might think it is, it's much worse. Especially when compared to any other "rich" nation. The more I learned about what passed for healthcare in America, the more bewildered I became. Unless you are military, or over sixty-five and eligible for Medicare, the American system of healthcare is designed to kill you. Well, more accurately, it is designed to take all of your money for as long as you remain reasonably healthy. Then if you get sick, it kills you.

It is organized crime—nothing more, nothing less. The only difference is that the U.S. government is complicit in the plundering and killing of its citizens. The intel started to come in on this lowlife in a three-thousand-dollar suit: Grant Pearson. Yes, he was only a figurehead for this multi-headed monster we call healthcare in America. For the first time since I started this life, I am genuinely pleased with my assignment and will chop his fucken head off with great pleasure. Well, not precisely chop his head off, but I will blow it off. In fact, I am going to make it my business to shoot him in his thieving, murderous face if I get the chance and if it doesn't endanger the mission.

Even doctors and nurses are victims of our demented system. They are swamped in artificially created paperwork and trapped within mazes and drowned with nonsense all designed to enrich the foreign shareholders of the HMO corporations and deny or delay healthcare to the Americans that pay the price.

If you sense anger on my part, you are wrong. I am not angry. But I am determined to destroy this monster and every other monster I can get within my scope. Never have I been more certain that I had made the right choice on the day I said yes to Jane.

The mission itself was not particularly challenging, but it was far away. Pearson was CEO and chairman of the board of the HMO Surety Health Insurance Technology. Yes, SHIT. And SHIT's headquarters and the head SHIThead's home was in Palo Alto, California. Which was in Silicon Valley. Mostly because this grifting lowlife tried to position his thieving, murdering company as a technology concern rather than the pretend healthcare administrators that they are. I would gladly spend the rest of my life repeatedly popping the people who might occupy his office once he's gone. That is if Jane would go for it, and I could bring Linda along.

Yes, it was far. More than three thousand miles far. And Jane still had an aversion to me and airports, so I started heading west immediately. It would take me more than five days to drive it. More than enough time for Jane to make all of her arrangements. I had encouraged her to find me more HMO scumbags to pop while I was out there. But her response had been unexpected.

"Just do the one, John. We will need some time to assess the results in ways I can't discuss. Just promise me that you won't go rogue. We will find other targets for you while you are out west, but not every one of them will be exciting, or serve any purpose you can immediately understand. So take this piece of shit as a sign of my gratitude for your good work, but I don't know yet just how far we can go with this . . . . Now is the part where you say, 'yes, ma'am.'"

I could understand what she was getting at and gave to her the much deserved "Yes, ma'am."

A nice part about the drive was that I had a lot of time to talk to Linda. We actually did talk on the phone a lot. Not just exchanging texts. She would be receiving her master's degree while I was away. I shared her excitement but was a bit bummed that I wouldn't be able to be there for the graduation ceremony. It was actually going to be a fairly low-key ceremony at Baruch College. But her parents would be attending, and I had hoped that it might be an opportunity to meet them. On the other hand, it might be for the best that I couldn't be there. I passed the time trying to imagine the introduction: "Mom, Dad, this is my boyfriend, John. He has no apparent job and disappears for weeks at a time." Yes, maybe it would be better to skip that for now.

As usual, we had plenty to talk about and I told her how incredibly proud I was of her for achieving this milestone.

"Does this mean no more coffee shop?" I asked.

She was cryptic in her response, joking that she wasn't sure if she was quite ready to grow up yet. "Besides," she quipped, "I might just decide to drop everything and travel the world with you, or wherever the fuck it is that you go."

This was one of the first times she ever referred to my erratic appearances and disappearances, even in jest. But I'm not going to lie, having her always by my side was appealing to me. Just as it remained completely impossible.

Again, I amused myself as I imagined a conversation from

our imagined life together: "I'll be back in a couple of hours, honey, I have to go kill this really wretched soon-to-be-former human being."

"OK, baby," she would answer in my imagination. "Don't miss!"

No, this wouldn't work out. I was always grateful that she rarely, if ever, put me in a position to have to lie to her. She did ask me where I was going but was perfectly satisfied with my honest answer, "California." She didn't ask why.

There were no further conversations with Jane. But the intel, arrangements, and instructions continued to pour into my phone and were complete long before I reached my destination.

Kate and I used this time to work through a few things that she thought could be potential issues. I got the sense that she really enjoyed talking to me, whether it was work related or otherwise. She knew I hadn't suffered any ill effects from my work with my first female "subject." Yet she delved into that area. She knew Linda and I were on solid ground, despite the tenuous, sporadic nature of our relationship. Yet she would find problems where neither I nor Linda seemed to. It seemed as if she were preparing me emotionally for a letdown that had shown no signs of coming. If I didn't know better, I might start to think that Kate had an agenda for me of her own. One that Linda was standing squarely in the way of. But that was impossible. I made a mental note to myself, basically thinking, "Who the fuck do you think you are?" My own ego had swelled and shrunk throughout this adventure. The low point being when I had hit nothing seven straight times during my first mission in New York. I think the all-time high was after I had put a hole in Jimmy Grahm's Bentley and Jimmy Grahm. But this was off the charts. I was Kate's job, perhaps her only job. Nothing more.

Pearson ended up being something of a letdown. It was almost too easy. I blew his stupid face off right in front of his fancy apartment building just outside Palo Alto. If I seem to be taking an inordinate amount of joy in his death, you are probably right. But the fact is that he, and those like him, are the worst human beings I can imagine. Murderers in suits. Yes, Forrest Reagan and his successor had been true genocidal maniacs. But in a way they seemed like outliers and cartoonishly evil. Pearson and those like him were very real and, in my mind at least, somehow worse for their common business-as-usual form of evil.

Jane didn't waste my trip to the west. The Bay Area of San Francisco and Oakland had a massive and surprisingly organized hierarchal drug trade. I spent more than a month there. I was moving constantly and executed fourteen of the fifteen leaders that Jane had requested. The other was killed by one of his own. The local clergy lost a couple of their most notorious but legally untouchable pedophiles. I got no thank-you note from the local parishioners. I spent almost the entire next month working my way south through California. I had never been to either San Diego or Los Angeles. I flirted with the idea of visiting Disneyland or Universal Studios or a bunch of other touristy things. But I realized that I would enjoy them much more if the time came that I could visit those places with Linda. See them through her eyes, feel them with her excitement. San Diego was among the most beautiful cities I have ever seen and had almost impossibly good weather. L.A. was a mixed bag of glamour, rampant homelessness, and traffic. San Francisco also had a widely visible homeless population, and I couldn't help but feel like I was seeing a preview of the future. A future where more and more Americans fall off the bottom rung of the economic ladder and onto the street. I would kill every Pearson piece of shit in the world to make that stop if it were within my power. But it wasn't.

I left a trail of dead drug dealers and various other misanthropes along my path. But no one else with the value of Pearson. At least not from my point of view. Which is and will always remain secondary to that of Jane.

Jane continued to keep me up to date on the ever-growing legend of The Silencer. The nebulous world of online commentary had decided that the demise of the Northern California drug kingpins had indeed been my handiwork. I chalked that up to the age-old theory that sometimes even a blind squirrel finds a nut. But Jane would never be so cavalier and probably had more concern for my safety and anonymity than I did for myself. So after almost two months out west, I was finally heading east.

For the first time since I had started, Jane had nowhere in particular for me to go. She told me that she was working on some things and that I'd be in an indefinite holding pattern. She wasn't sure. It might only be a day or two, or it could be a week or more. I had an idea and at this point there was no reason to be coy about it.

"What do you say I fly Linda out to Vegas for a few days and meet her out there? I've never been, and if I've got some time to kill . . ."

"I'm sorry, John," she replied, "but this could change on a moment's notice." I could tell from her tone that she was definitely sympathetic. "I don't mind if you head that way, that's fine. But I can't have you needing to explain if you have to get out of there in a hurry. I promise you there will be other opportunities."

I was disappointed, but I really did understand. I knew that Houston would still be on the agenda at some point, but other than that I had no idea what was coming next. With Jane's blessing I started driving toward Las Vegas. Why not? I'd never been there. The only casino I'd ever been to was the Indian one back in Allset, and I never even went in the actual casino. I've never done any kind of gambling, and it held exactly zero interest for me. Winning or losing money would have no impact on my life either way. I suppose there might be a competitive element to playing blackjack or poker that might be interesting, but not interesting enough to actually try it. If I were to play, I would at least want to have some idea of what I was doing. I would go down the rabbit hole of trying to learn everything there is to know, and it just wasn't worth the time. Still it would be fun to check the place out for a couple of days or until Jane sent me packing.

I booked a room at a resort near the center of the Las Vegas Strip called Paris. I figured I could walk pretty much everywhere from there and I was right. It's a nice place to visit but I wouldn't want to live there. There really were a lot of cool things to see but I couldn't help but wish that Linda was here with me to see it.

I did finally put twenty dollars in a slot machine just to see what it was like. It was, in fact, a lot like taking a twenty-dollar bill, tearing it up, pissing on it, waiting for it to dry, and then setting it on fire. More directly, you put money in, push a button, and the money goes away. It's not at all like I have seen in the movies. In reality, it is row after row of mostly very overweight people feeding bills into a slot and pushing a button. It's supposed to be fun, but almost nobody I saw playing was smiling. Overall, it looked like a pretty grim affair. But the machines themselves were colorful and interesting. They were truly marvels of technology. Me being me, I couldn't help myself. I spent more than three hours in my room learning about the history of slot machines, then several more learning about the entire industry. Damn if I didn't find the same type of bug that seems to crawl out from pretty much every rock I turn over.

Giant multinational corporations had come to dominate an industry that had once been run fairly honestly by the mafia. By comparison, the gamblers got a much better shake from the mafia.

There are dozens of massive resorts on the strip. Yet almost all are owned by only three corporations. Gambling offers the illusion of choice where almost none exists. Gone are the days of good cheap food, free or cheap entertainment, and free parking. Today the "guest" is squeezed out of every nickel, often before they can even make the seat warm as they mindlessly press the button over and over.

Don't get me wrong, Vegas is fun. There is plenty to do and see without betting a nickel. I really enjoyed Red Rock, a national park not too far away. It was breathtaking in its beauty, and I went there for my run/walk a few times. There was also Mount Charleston less than an hour away. Starting out at the bottom, the temperature was close to a hundred degrees. Once you got to the top, it was dry but below freezing. And there were patches of snow on the ground. It was awesome, and only less so because I was without Linda by my side to experience it with me.

But again, just like everywhere I cared to look, the jaws of corporate oligarchy had slammed shut on Las Vegas, destroying meaningful free market competition and manipulating the government to its own benefit. That didn't mean I was going to wander around popping casino executives. It just added one more piece to the puzzle that was our democracy under assault by financial forces so powerful that no government could hope to contain it. Unless they had us, I thought with some small hope.

I had read an analogy, and forgive me for not remembering the original author, that said "Capitalism is the greatest beast of burden ever created. When properly yoked it brings wealth and prosperity to all. But if left to run wild it will shit all over everything and eat your children." It doesn't take a genius to understand her meaning. Capitalism, when well regulated as part of a healthy democracy, is the best of all possible worlds. Unregulated, it is destructive and will "shit all over everything and eat your children." That is pretty much where we are now. Our job, well Jane's job with my eager assistance, is to restore capitalism and free markets, preferably before lunch if possible.

I had almost a week before my mission orders started filtering through, and these were some mission orders indeed. My first politician. I was to start working my way toward Austin, the capital of Texas. Houston's drug dealers got yet another temporary reprieve. I was on my way the same day.

NINETEEN

Ah, Texas. There is nowhere in the world quite like it. I had been there a few months earlier to take care of my business with the now late Jimmy Grahm. But I had spent most of my time in rather ritzy Houston suburbs, so I won't even pretend to know a whole lot about this massive and surprisingly diverse state. This time I was heading for Austin. The capital is itself an outlier within the state. It's known for art, music, cultural, sexual diversity, and of course, the state capitol. It was also home to The University of Texas at Austin. It was a huge, sprawling university with well over fifty thousand students.

Yet even in this town crawling with young people, I still couldn't help but notice how ridiculously fat almost everybody was. Look, I'm not fat shaming and I have nothing intrinsically against overweight people. But my experience and travel over the last few months has led me to the conclusion that the insane weight of the American public was epidemic to the point that it should be declared a national emergency.

I had said as much to Jane whose immediate response was, "Who the fuck are you to say. Mind your own business." But this kneejerk response was followed by a softer and more well-considered reply, "You're not wrong, John, but when you look at this problem you will realize that it is intertwined with a whole bunch of other ones. Some of which do fall within our purview. For instance, did you know that more than half of men over forty are taking drugs called statins?"

"No," I replied. "What does that mean?"

"A lot, unfortunately," she answered. "And this is no exaggeration. Statins make you stupid and, even worse, they have almost no benefit for what they're supposed to do, which is reduce cholesterol and cardiac problems for people with high cholesterol. They do one thing really well though. Pharmaceutical companies make twenty billion dollars a year selling them, mostly to dopey white men over forty, and then the drug makes them even dopier. You can buy an awful lot of votes with twenty billion dollars. Even better, you can buy a lot of sway with the FDA to keep the scam going."

Jesus Christ, I thought but didn't say aloud. Another rock with another disgusting creature crawling out from underneath it. Another huge, mostly foreign-owned group of corporate douchebags finger fucking Americans. I knew better than to push any further on this subject because I knew we had a specific mission. But I wasn't going to let this go. If I had any say whatsoever, Jane would be pointing me in their direction sooner or later.

For now, the danger was real, immediate, and particularly silly. Jane had asked me to, so I had done some background research on secessionist movements in U.S. history. There was of course the Civil War. But beyond that there had been numerous smaller and less remembered events. There had also been numerous debates in dozens of states that had never amounted to much of anything but talk. For the record, my favorite was the tongue-in-cheek secessionist movement in Key

West, Florida, that, in an alternate universe, would have brought about "The Conch Republic."

Throughout its history, Texas had flirted on and off with talk of secession. But what was going on now was an entirely different animal. A formerly little-known state legislator named Josh Cruz had built up quite a following with seemingly endless television appearances. He spoke always about how "Texas values" were no longer compatible with the "elitist pedophile values" of Washington, and it was the "Christian" duty of Texas to secede. In a world where ironic stupidity is always the soup of the day, this particular moron still stood out. Without evidence or even the slightest element of reality, he would continually call out these imaginary "Washington pedophile elites." Just in case there wasn't quite enough irony, this dickface had never once publicly mentioned the thousands of pedophile clergy that had been investigated, convicted, and sent to jail with actual evidence. Tens of thousands of victims had been identified and equally well documented. But this never warranted any public mention by Cruz because it would reflect poorly on the Christian values that his version of Texas embraced but the Washington elites ignored.

This would all be OK. Our history is full of jerkoffs like this and a good bit worse. The part that spooked Jane is that he was gaining traction, and a lot of it. There was even more irony. Jane was pretty sure that Cruz had no interest in actual secession. Rather it was just a way to attract attention and name recognition in his run for U.S. Senate the next year. But honest or not, it was becoming dangerously real. Jane really did shy away from politics as much as she could. But if the Texas legislature actually passed articles of secession, it could lead to other states doing the same. It had the potential to unleash chaos, widespread violence, and even the possibility of an actual civil war. She wasn't willing to take that risk. This guy had to go.

This would be an unusual assignment beyond it being my

first politician. Jane wanted to figure out how to make it convincingly look like an accident. So a public bullet through his skull wouldn't do.

Jane spent the next week combing through intel, and I spent that time shadowing him from a discreet distance. What I came up with was pretty safe, but not one hundred percent certain to get the job done. On his way home, Cruz would cross several bridges over various bodies of water, none of which had guardrails. After all, this was Texas. Why build guardrails and safe roads when you could use that money to give subsidies to the corporate sponsors that fund your campaign? Some of these bridges had very safe places for me to set up nearby, and the water below was deep enough for Fuckface to drown if he lost control of the vehicle.

Definitely not a sure thing. But I felt confident that if I could get this three hundred pounder and his late model Mercedes into the water, he wouldn't emerge alive. I did some studying on my secure tablet about how to shoot a tire in the right way to get the vehicle to go the way you want it to. It was a fairly simple matter, though still not foolproof. A lot would depend on how he reacted after the blowout. The bullet would pass through the tire, and it would surely appear to have been a blowout.

Again, not to toot my own horn, but it worked perfectly. I shot out the rear back tire and it looked like he jerked the wheel violently to the right. The car skidded sideways and fell over, turning directly upside down as it hit the water. It remained bobbing in the water upside down for almost a minute before sliding under the surface, front end first. I watched through my scope for any signs of his escape, but there was none.

Josh Cruz, the wannabe father of a new and wretched nation, drowned to death upside down and still in his seatbelt. The official investigations were opened and closed. The car had suffered a blowout. And fatass couldn't get out of the car fast enough to save his life. The world is now a better place without him.

Jane was thrilled with the result. The secessionist movement was not quite dead but took quite a few steps back from the brink. Despite others trying to rally their equally portly troops by trying to cast him as a martyr to the cause, it had lost its sustaining momentum. There was no suspicion of it having been an assassination, and life would go on. She was so certain of my safety that I was sent to Houston to clear up my unfinished business there.

The drug lords of Houston were a particularly nasty bunch and dangerous to match. I have nothing against Mexicans, but the gatekeepers here were all members of the same extended Mexican family. And all of them, almost without exception, were extremely violent, vengeful, and efficient. These were some brutal fuckers. It was not at all unusual for them to attack families of innocents rather than use their own false front businesses to launder money. This group would strong-arm legitimate businesses into doing their bidding, killing family members of the owners simply to make the point that it was better to cooperate with them in laundering many millions of dollars.

I was glad that I had been diverted from them some months ago. Not that I lacked confidence, but this was an unusually competent, sophisticated, and close-knit organization. Not to mention very well armed. Learning about this group had made me realize how the drug cartels of Mexico had gained so much corrupt political power. There was irony in that this level of competence would probably have made them successful in legitimate business if they had wanted that. But these were career criminals, sometimes second, third, or even fourth generation. They knew no other life. It made me sad that such talent could not be used for good. And the thought crossed my mind that in Jane's world without need, such people and organizations would not exist. One of countless ways that a fed, clothed, and homed world would be different, and much, much better.

To completely destroy this cartel would be a full-time job for years if Jane truly wanted it gone. The list of potential targets was close to a hundred. There was no way I could take out that many experienced and cunning criminals without eventually drawing attention to myself. We were also aware that these were extremely resourceful people who would surely devise ways to protect themselves once the shootings started. I might get two or three before the rest would submerge or cross the border into Mexico. This is where the true genius of Jane became apparent. I'm not sure how she did it, but she directed me through a series of targets that caused the organization to practically go to war with itself.

I took out only eight very strategically chosen targets over a period of almost six weeks. But the final body count ended up being closer to fifty. All but my eight they had inflicted on themselves. Jane had somehow figured out how to exploit the various factions that exist within every organization. I get no credit for any of that. All I did was take out each target at the exact time I was instructed to. Jane and the bad guys did the rest.

Did we destroy the drug trade in Houston? No, not even close. But we did raise the cost of their doing business. Both in blood and money. This would be a long-term project, and there was no doubt in my mind that I would be back, probably in a year or less.

I decided that, after all my hard work, I was going to put my foot down with Jane and demand a vacation and some uninterrupted time with Linda. That lasted for all of about eight seconds into the conversation. I started by saying that I was going to New York City to see Linda. Not just going but flying. It was my estimation that I had driven about fifty thousand miles and dammit, I deserved the chance to fly to New York and see my girlfriend while I still had one. In reality it was more than eight seconds because Jane allowed me to finish my complete rant before answering.

"You done?" she asked with exaggerated politeness and didn't wait for me to answer before continuing, "Yes, John, you are going to New York, but I'm only a little sorry to say you will be driving again. We are going to continue our little experiment in the Capital District. Then you can go to the city and see your girlfriend. But I'm not sure for how long yet. If that's not fair enough, I genuinely apologize. But you agreed to this life, and I think I gave you a completely honest description before you signed up. True or false?"

I didn't answer right away, but she was actually right, which at the moment, I found particularly annoying. "Yes," I finally admitted.

"Good!" she replied. "Because I'm exhausted," she said with a laugh. "But you have a good, long vacation coming up pretty soon. You can only pop so many people before even stupid people can start connecting the dots, so you're going to have to go out of circulation for a while."

"Yeah, I get it," I replied.

I had already figured this was coming. Let's face it, there was a sequential trail of dead bodies from Northern California to Southern California and east back to Houston. It made perfect sense.

"So what do you mean by vacation?" I asked. "Well, at least a couple of months in New Mexico. Your training was cut short a little bit. You could do with some refreshers and definitely some more language work. But there should be some time for you to travel after that if you want to. We'll see how it plays out."

The more I thought about it, the more I realized that Jane

had indeed been playing fair with me throughout this whole venture. There was nothing that happened that she hadn't prepared me for or told me about before any of this started. In fact, my having any kind of relationship with Linda could be considered an indulgence. Certainly, from Jane's point of view. She had all but told me that a romantic relationship of any kind would be nearly impossible. Yet Linda and I had somehow managed to pull it off, so far at least. We were still speaking quite a bit. Texting often and even a little bit of sexting of a sort. Though I still had stopped short of ever sending a dick pic.

TWENTY

I definitely knew my way to the Capital District. This really was a behavioral experiment with much larger implications. Jane wanted to see what would happen if you repeatedly beheaded a criminal organization. What changes, if any, would occur? Would using the same tactics on a legal but corrupt organization change or stop their behavior?

She had selected that area for a specific reason as well. It was a large enough market to have a cohesive "management" of the drug trade, but small enough to be—how can I put this?—realistically killable. Meaning it wasn't like Houston where I couldn't kill anywhere near enough people to make much of an observable difference. Neither of us had any illusions that we could stop people from buying and using drugs. There will always be a market. And as long as they remain illegal, they will always spawn criminal organizations. Historians agree that prohibition of alcohol had spawned modern organized crime in America. The war on drugs just created even more crime, more powerful criminals, and more corruption. It's not a stretch to say that the war on drugs was also more of a war on black people. I had studied the issue extensively and had come to the conclusion that drug laws' main purpose was to imprison and disenfranchise black people and later to fill private prisons with profitable prisoners, again, most of them black. I had discussed this with Jane on more than one occasion because it was so shitty in so many ways. She had agreed with my conclusions. She had even joked that there was a reason that people like us sociopaths were not racist—we hate everybody equally. I hoped that was a joke. But her agreement didn't necessarily mean we were going to take action to change things. Or at least no action that involved me yet. It was entirely possible that she was fighting that war on another front using other pieces on the chess board that I know nothing about.

I hoped that all of this would lead her, and me, onto bigger and more meaningful targets. If it was up to me, we would be popping what I had started calling "Crappers," the people from Creating Real American Progress. To me, these assholes have done more damage to this country than every drug dealer and every thieving preacher that ever lived combined. They were the common element that tied so many of the other problems together. They are literally corruption incarnate. I had brought this up with Jane a bunch of times and had been rebuked every time.

Maybe I was naïve to believe that just going to CRAP headquarters in Bentonville and killing everybody would solve the world's problems. But I knew one thing for sure, it couldn't hurt.

Again, Jane agreed but deferred. "We would be starting a war," she told me again, "one we are not yet ready to win."

I'm not going to say that I hurried my assignments in New York, but I didn't waste any time. I knew that as soon as I was finished, I would be able to return to New York City to see Linda.

Since she had graduated, she'd taken on a couple of extra days at the coffee shop. In her words, she was just "killing time" until figuring out what, if anything, she wanted to do with her advanced degree. I had indeed offered her money for any show tickets she might want, but she refused to take it.

"John, I don't want to sound ungrateful because that's really, really sweet of you," she said. "But I won't take money from any man that's not my father, even you."

I protested, saying that I knew how much she loved Broadway and I just wanted to see her enjoy things and be, you know, happy. I think she understood that, but in her mind, it could hurt our relationship, and she said as much.

"Money just fucks things up, John. Don't get me wrong, if I were starving and you threw me a bone, I would take it. I'm not stupid. But it's just better if we don't throw money into things. It only screws things up. Besides, I would rather see the shows with you. Especially if you hate them," she joked.

I actually understood what that meant. If I watched the show with her, even if I hated them, it would show that I really cared. I was a bit surprised that she noticed my indifference to the one show we had seen together. I had smiled when you were supposed to smile and applauded when you were supposed to clap. But I didn't fool her. She knew I had been at least a little bit bored. As usual, the women of my life were at least a couple of steps ahead of me, a fact that I was getting used to and more than comfortable with.

Rushing didn't help. The drug trade had not stopped with the continuous demise of its leaders. Instead, it had fragmented. There were now more, but fewer leaders with as much power. It had declined into a series of small fiefdoms. Multiple dealers had emerged to control smaller and smaller areas. I was proud of this work. In a strange way we had "democratized" the drug business in the Capital District. The dealers now seemed to sense that bigger was not necessarily better. Bigger might mean dead. Instead of a handful of powerful criminals, we now had dozens of less powerful criminals. That mattered, especially to Jane's experiment. People still bought drugs and people still sold them. But there was no central power, no person or group powerful enough to dominate, or worse, corrupt public officials. In a strange way, it had worked. That didn't stop Jane from giving me twenty—yes, twenty—targets. The deal was that once I got any ten of them of my choosing I could stop and head for New York City and Linda. Fair enough. It took almost three weeks, but I gave her a bonus hit. Ten and eleven were together at the time, so I popped both.

In my opinion, at least, the experiment in the Capital District had been wildly successful. Simply put, if we killed enough bad people things would get better. The relatively small-time dealers that remained didn't have the reach or power to buy off or intimidate cops, judges, or politicians. In my mind, this should work for the corporate criminals just as it would with street thugs. If we killed every Grant Pearson and any replacements, eventually something had to give. There would be no one left crazy enough to want these jobs that had become death sentences. This would cause power to drift and diffuse within the organization. There would be no more Imperial Grand Poohbahs. Financial decisions would come from groups of people who would have to face each other rather than from a single elite person who answered only to shareholders. Would it make enough difference to change the murderous habits of the healthcare industry? I don't know. And even if it did work, it would still require constant vigilance to prevent power from reconsolidating in either the streets of New York or the executive suites of Palo Alto. But I do know it couldn't possibly make things any worse. I also know that I am still game to find out.

Fuck all of that. I was on my way to see my girl. I considered it something of a happy miracle that she was still my girl. I have always had at least average confidence in myself and, if anything, I was overconfident in some areas. Even that being true doesn't change the fact that I still think Linda is too good for me. On paper, I haven't been able to give this woman anywhere near what she deserves out of a man. It's certainly not because I didn't want to. But I had a job I had promised to do. Walking away was not an option I could even consider. I'm not sure that I would even live if I walked away. Jane had said strongly from day one that it was more likely than not to be a one-way ticket. I didn't want to know what it might mean if I were to break my promise.

For now, I would give Linda everything I had to give and just pray that it would be enough. I had left all the hardware back upstate and traveled clean. For the first time I got to stay with Linda in her apartment. Both of her flight attendant roommates were out of town, and we had the apartment to ourselves.

Again, it felt like we picked up exactly where we had left off. We fit neatly together in the city, in her apartment, and in her bed. I arrived the first night after 10 p.m. and Linda had to work the next morning at 6:30. That didn't stop us from hungrily "laying all over" each other all night, the grand finale coming in her shower as she prepared for work at about a quarter to six.

"You're simply determined to never let me get any sleep, aren't you?" she asked as she finished dressing for work.

She somehow managed to look pretty well put together for a woman on her way to work without having had even a minute of sleep. For my part I slept only a couple of hours after she left for the day. I was determined to fall asleep that night with her in my arms and on more or less the same sleep schedule.

I spent the day gathering what I needed to prepare dinner so it would be ready when she got home from work. I knew she would be exhausted, both from the calisthenics of the early morning followed by a nine-hour shift on her feet at the coffee shop. I didn't want to get too over the top schmaltzy. But I prepared a four-course meal. OK, "prepared" might be too strong a word because it started with a bagged salad. But then there was fresh broccoli and cauliflower with a cheese sauce, chicken breast prepared with a lime and mojo sauce that I sort of invented, and I topped it all off with a chocolate chip cannoli for each of us. The cannoli came from her favorite Italian deli a couple of blocks down, and I knew it was her favorite. There were also two bottles of her favorite red wine. Last but not least was a single candle that I placed in the center of our table for two that I lit two minutes before she got home at exactly 5:15. She was taking her shoes off as she walked through the door. For a brief moment I thought she was going to throw one of them at me, but she stopped suddenly, sniffed a couple of times and said, "Something smells nice," and then added, "and I know it's not you."

Not to brag, but I knew that I had pulled off a beautifully romantic dinner for an extremely tired and still beautiful woman. We ate largely in silence, but I could tell she was impressed, and I was quite boyishly proud of myself.

We finished one of the bottles with dinner and were about to open the second when she said, "Let's save that one for tomorrow night." Then she just looked at me across the table for what felt like forever but was probably no more than a few seconds. Finally, she asked with a hint of sarcasm to her voice, "You're ridiculously proud of yourself, aren't you?" She didn't wait for me to answer, looking directly in my eyes, and without the slightest hint of irony she said, "You should be proud, John, this was amazing." After a time she added, "And you're gonna give me the recipe for that chicken or I'll kill ya." And she laughed.

In that moment I almost knew what it felt like to be a "normal" person. I had made the woman I valued very, very happy. If only for the moment. That was more than enough for me.

Shockingly, there was a show she wanted to see the next night. Another musical. It was sold out, but we managed to scalp some pretty good seats at four hundred bucks a pop. The show was amazing. Spectacular pyrotechnics and sets, memorable songs, and magnificent acting. There was so much talent that went into this production that they made me feel like a talentless schlub. I put this thought aside, knowing that all of us have talent of different kinds. Sometimes more, sometimes less. But everyone had something. For instance, I was talented at killing shitty people, usually from a great distance. That was more than nothing. And the truth is that aside from the victims themselves, the world had benefitted quite a bit from my work. I took no joy in that. It isn't a brag. It is simply true.

Linda loved the show, but I had the feeling that I may have liked it even more than she did. And now she had another Playbill to add to her collection. We headed toward her favorite pastry shop for a little post-show dessert. We were happy, maybe more than ever, and walking the streets of New York City without a care.

I knew better. Life, even my life, did not need to be lived with guns drawn. But life, especially my life, had to be lived with the constant attention and vigilance that Jane had tried to introduce to me that very first day at Chipotle.

This was definitely not the case as we turned a corner, and I immediately received a poorly thrown punch that still landed full force on my forehead just below my hairline. I was stunned, but for only for a few moments. On the other end of that punch was a bearded man that I judged to be Russian, or at the very least Eastern European. He was holding a small American-made handgun whose brand I could not tell. But I was pretty sure the weapon was unloaded or at the very least unprepared to fire because the slide lock was closed. His origins were confirmed when he said with a thick Russian accent, "I will have that purse, bitch," to Linda. He followed up with, "and your wallet," gesturing to me.

Linda, of course, had instinctively taken three of four steps back when I was punched and she was now a few feet from our attacker who had stayed close to me, obviously considering me the greater threat. In a way I was relieved. If this were an assassination attempt and I was getting popped, it would certainly have happened already. No, this was a simple attempted mugging. I say attempted because, as Linda retrieved her purse, she pulled a comically tiny handgun from the purse and used it to take dead aim at our would-be mugger. With my training, I recognized it instantly as a Glock 43, a model popular with women for its small size, modest kickback, and impressive power for its size.

The Russian saw this and turned his weapon to point at me, as he himself took a couple of steps back from us. "Maybe I just kill him?" he asked in what was a last attempt to salvage at least something out of this botched operation.

"Yeah, that would be a problem," Linda said. "We both know that your weapon isn't ready to fire," she continued. "I'm not sure how much English you understand, but I suggest you get the fuck away from us before I have to kill you, which would be a real pain in the ass."

A very confused look came across his face. I wasn't sure if it was because he really didn't understand English very well or if it was because he understood it all too well. I will never know for sure, as he shoved the gun in his jacket pocket and took off running down the street. In that moment, I was convinced that the absolute sexiest woman in the history of the universe was standing in front of me.

"Apparently there is much more to you than meets the eye," I said. She showed only the slightest signs of having been being rattled by the experience. She ignored the question and gently reached out to my face where I'd been punched.

"Are you OK?" she asked with an almost motherly sincerity.

"I'm a little scared," I lied. "But it doesn't really hurt, I'm pretty sure I'll survive," I said with a smile.

"You can never be too careful," she said, adding, "My father made me promise when I moved to New York that I would learn how to protect myself. I took a few classes and then bought this little cutie right here." She gestured to the Glock, now back in her purse but still partially visible.

I wasn't certain, but I was pretty sure that it was illegal to carry any form of handgun in New York City. But I didn't bring it up. As a man. I cannot hope to understand the vulnerability and fears of women. When you look at the numbers, which of course I had, some absurdly high percentage of woman had suffered some type of sexual abuse during their lifetimes. Those numbers were rising with each new batch of research, and I had often pondered why that was so. Was rape of women and sexual abuse of children rising to epidemic levels? Or was it simply the result that women and children felt more able to report the incidents? It was one of the bizarre elements of human behavior that we somehow blame ourselves when we have been abused this way. Little boys and girls were similar in their tendency to turn the blame of their own abuse on themselves. Blame that, from any other observer, would appear clearly as a grotesque act of horrible violence against those least able to defend themselves. I had finally concluded that the problem was not, in fact, getting any worse or widespread. I think that it had just become more visible as more victims became felt more empowered to report their attackers and pursue them legally. This was a good thing. And some of the most satisfying actions of my own work came when I was able to remove from the earth any of these repulsive animals, way too many of whom came shrouded in the cloak of godliness.

Linda seemed OK. And I thought I had at least appeared rattled enough to seem like a "normal" person reacting to a terrifying incident. Not that I had been completely unaffected. This fucker had punched me and pointed his weapon at me. The fact that I was near certain that the gun wasn't loaded definitely helped me to take it all in stride. But near certain is not certain, and I'd be lying if I said that my blood pressure hadn't gone up a bit, if only momentarily.

But we didn't let it ruin the rest of our evening. Neither of us even mentioned calling the police. There was no point. I think it was just a desperate nutbag thinking he had an easy target. I tried my joke with Linda that no one had ever laughed at, but I enjoy it, so I said it anyway. "That guy is not only not playing with a full deck" I said. "He's only playing with the four of clubs."

I fully expected the blank stare that came from Linda in response to my joke.

"Putz," she said, gesturing to me and shaking her head. "Pretty cute, but a putz."

We went for a late dinner at a diner and returned to her apartment to "lay all over" each other and kill that other bottle of wine.

There was no contact from Jane or Kate, which was just fine by me. Every day I didn't hear from them meant another day in our personal paradise. We didn't do much of anything for the next couple of days. We took long walks in Central Park, splurged on a wildly expensive lunch at Tavern on the Green. It was good, but for that kind of money, it should have come with a reach around between courses. I said as much to Linda, who replied, "Sorry, baby, I can't reach from here."

As was becoming customary, I couldn't be a hundred percent sure she wasn't kidding. Had she been seated next to me rather than across the table, I could easily envision her calmly jerking me off under the table as we sat surrounded by other customers.

The more amazing part was Central Park itself. It was a beautiful, natural, giant oasis in one of the most densely populated places on Earth. It made me sad to realize that I could not imagine any modern American politicians with the vision that it would take to create something like that now. It would be completely impossible. Yet I couldn't help but think about the untold millions of people who had enjoyed that island of green in the middle of the concrete jungle of that was New York City.

On the fifth day, I started to receive intel from Jane, and I knew that the clock was now ticking. It wouldn't be long before I was pulled away from the woman and place that now meant so much to me. I have to give Jane some much deserved credit. And Kate for that matter as well. They had left me alone, completely untouched for five days. There was no way to look at it except as an act of kindness. There is no doubt in my mind that she could easily have found something for me to do during those five days. But they had left me completely alone. I almost felt like a "normal" person. Or at least as normal as I could ever be.

TWENTY-ONE

Two more assignments. I had just two more assignments before I would be pulled out of circulation. As Jane had said, "out of circulation" meant two things: training and vacation. I expected something like my original days of training. Frequent visits and video calls and some days free to do what I please. I had not yet asked the most important question. Maybe because I was afraid that I might not like the answer. Would it be possible for Linda to be with me in New Mexico? Or would that be too risky and untenable? I honestly wasn't sure what answer I would get from Jane. It was a sure thing that she knew the question was coming. It was just a matter of who would bring it up first. Would Linda want to hang out with me in the middle of nowhere with no good explanation as to why we were there? Would it even be possible to do the things I needed to do with her around? For now, there was work to do and I would wait as long as I could to pose the question.

My "two assignments" didn't necessarily mean two targets. The first assignment was a whole new arena, and I was quite pleased to be involved. Jane had not offered a lot of background about the targets other than the locations, names, and photos. But it didn't take much research to figure out what was going on.

"So we're going after climate science deniers now, are we," I said to Jane, more statement than question.

"Yes, but aren't you being a bit vain to think we're the only ones working on this?"

This was a bit surprising. Jane had never referred to anyone else she had in the field, and I never asked. The targets were all scientists that worked as paid shills for the oil companies. My own research quickly revealed that the major oil companies knew about climate change as early as 1970. In 1980, a scientist working for one of the largest oil companies actually invented the first lithium ion battery, technology we're just getting around to deploying now. They could have literally saved the world and dominated the market, but instead they fired the scientist (who actually went on to win a Nobel Prize for the work) and diverted their resources to funding bullshit studies with paid shill scientists to deny the existence of climate change.

Again, I am not one to throw the word "evil" around lightly. As my own life shows, a whole lot depends on your point of view. Not this time. This was some outright evil shit. They knew the problem before anyone else. They had a perfectly good solution before anyone else that would have made them mountains of money, but they still chose to quash the technology and destroy the only fucken planet where anyone could actually spend that mountain of money that they make. Evil. Now we are left with a pool of asshole scientists who still pretend climate change does not exist, even as the world around us boils before our eyes. They are employed by the oil companies in the most thinly veiled way, once again including our dear friends in Saudi Arabia. Jane has decided that it is time for several of them to exit the conversation—and the planet. None of the targets were, in fact, Saudis. As far as I could tell there were no Saudi climate scientists, even fake ones to whore for the oil giants. I guess if you are the Saudis, and you have dominated, corrupted, and terrorized the world with oil money for over a century, why bother with science? Religion serves their purposes much more reliably.

There was to be a roundtable debate about climate science as part of a larger scientific conference in where else? Houston. The conference would go on for over a month in a suburb of Houston known as The Woodlands. Again I was offered a buffet of targets, and I could choose which to pop based on expedience, availability, and my own safety. I took this as a compliment from Jane. It was a sign that she was able to rely on my judgment. She never said so explicitly, but it was hard to see it any other way. The parameters were pretty simple. I had a list of twenty targets. I was to take out as many as I could safely manage within a three-day window—two days if possible. Anything more than three targets popped was a bonus. Jane and I both understood that if I stayed too long, the jaws would clamp down. The targets would disappear and, even if I was shifting locations, each shooting would bring worldwide media coverage. There was a small window, and I was to make the most of it and then get the hell out of there.

The point of this, I gathered, was similar to that of our work in the Capital District and Palo Alto. If you wanted to use your scientific talents to make a living shilling for the oil giants and the Saudis, there may be a price to pay. Killing a few of these lowlifes wouldn't fix the world. But in the larger sense it may help more people learn what Jane, myself, and the entire legitimate scientific community already know: We are fucked. The question is just how fucked.

I was given a variety of locations to work from. Each came equipped with the gear I would need. I was two gigs from vacation, so I was determined to limit my own exposure as much as possible. That was how I always worked, but I was just a little more cautious than usual. I didn't go out much. There was no reason for anyone to see my face, even in passing. I did quite a bit of surveillance, the goal being to find a way to pop as many as possible as quickly as I could.

I was a little bit smart and a little bit lucky. I got two at one time on one day in the same place. And then another two at the same time later that night before media and law enforcement had much of a chance to descend on the area. It was probably my best and most efficient mission to date. Even better, it was for about as good a cause as I could imagine. Yes, I had been responsible for saving the lives of virtually every black person on earth, and I was proud of that. This work helped in some small way to save the Earth itself. Saving, at least in some small way, everyone.

I sent Jane the traditional text, "Done." She responded with her own one-word text, "Bye." That meant what I already knew and was already doing—getting the hell out of there. There was no immediate intel or instruction for what my second mission would be, so I just picked a direction at random and drove north until the sun came up the next day.

Texas being Texas, I was still within its borders. But not by much, and far from the mayhem in the suburbs of Houston.

Once I got settled in, I got Jane on the phone. I was only halfway kidding when I suggested that I wasn't too far away from the CRAPpers of Bentonville and that I would be more than happy to head over and "clean up a little bit."

Her answer to my "joke" was a bit more than I expected. "Look, dipshit," she began, "I know you are eager, and to tell the God's honest truth, so am I. But this is simply something we cannot do. Not yet. Let me spell it out for you because it appears nothing less will do. If you start going after them, you are a dead man, and it might even be me who has to make that happen. The full force of the corporate oligarchy would come down on you, and worse yet, me and my organization. And all of the good we have been doing would end, forever. Does that about cover it for you, or should I remind you again about the dangers of developing a god complex? Because you, my dear nephew, are well on your way."

I knew before she was halfway through her speech that I had stepped over the line, and I felt stupid for having basically badgered her into reprimanding me. She ended the conversation by telling me to just sit tight for a couple of days and she would soon be ready with the details of my next assignment.

It was no surprise at all that the next phone call was Kate. It was a hundred percent certain that Jane had directed her to call as soon as she hung up with me. I imagined an annoyed Jane telling Kate to please calm down her moron nephew, or something to that effect.

Kate knew me all too well. "I'm betting that I really don't need to tell you what I'm still obligated to tell you," she said, just after saying hello, which these days was a nice but unexpected touch. "Your aunt is dealing with a lot of things that neither you nor I know about and probably never will. The one thing that she wants to know is that she can depend on you."

"You're right," I replied, "on both parts." And then I added something that I didn't even realize myself until I said it out loud. "It's just that, for the first time, I'm starting to understand all of the good we're doing. And knowing that makes me want to do more."

I could almost feel her smile across the miles. "That's a good thing, John, it's a really good thing. But even good things can turn bad when it gets to be too much. It won't be long before you're out of circulation for a while. How are you going to handle that if you think you should be charging off to save the world like some demented white knight?"

Something about the phrase "demented white knight" made me laugh.

She waited a few seconds before adding, "Can you see my point?"

"Yes, ma'am," I replied, "even through my dementia. The truth is I'm ready for some training and some down time. It may not seem like it sometimes, but I know full well that I have a lot to learn if I want to have a long career."

"Let me ask you a question, Kate. What do you think Jane would say if I told her that I wanted Linda with me in New Mexico?"

There was a long pause. "John, I honestly don't know and, what's more, I'm not comfortable trying to advise you about that. But I would ask you, do you think it's the right thing to do? Is it the smart thing to do? I'm not telling you not to even ask, but I think you would be wise to really think it through before deciding if and when to pop that question to your aunt."

For someone who didn't feel comfortable, she sure had a lot to say on the matter. And it didn't do anything to lessen my creeping suspicion that Kate had an interest in me that went beyond the professional.

"John, you have done amazing work, better than anyone could've expected for someone so young and with such limited training," Kate said, before adding slyly, "And we owe it all to the hard work and dedication of your wildly talented and tireless counselor."

I replied with a grandly, "And I want to thank the Academy . . ." as if I were accepting an Oscar on her behalf.

The mission orders started coming in the next day. That was more than fine with me because I was literally in the middle of nowhere in a shitty motel. I was somewhere in the general vicinity of Oklahoma, if not actually in Oklahoma. I just saw signs that said, "Chickasaw Nation." Which means I had probably at some point passed the border out of Texas.

"Start heading toward New Orleans" was the first of my mission orders and I was more than happy to oblige. I'd never been to New Orleans, and it had always seemed like an interesting place. An island of debauchery in an otherwise very southern state.

I was pleased when I learned what the mission was. SHIT was on our radar again. The new president and CEO of Surety Health Insurance Technology was working out of New Orleans. She had stepped in temporarily for the recently deceased Grant Pearson, who I imagined as somewhere in the afterlife every bit still the douche he had been during his visit to Earth. This was a buy-one-get-one-free deal. I was going to pop Pearson's replacement. Cristina Van Den Shultz. An elderly woman and the matriarch of the Van Den Shultz family. That family had founded this delightful organization some fifty years ago. She herself was just a placeholder for her would-be heir apparent and son Donald Shultz. He had legally dropped the "Van Den" from his name some time ago for reasons unknown. And I couldn't work up anywhere near enough "give a shit" to want to know why. The point was that these two were easily as despicable as their predecessor and possibly even worse. They had made public announcements to reassure jittery shareholders and Wall Street in general. They boldly predicted the companies "best quarter ever," now that family leadership had been restored. We all know there is only one way for an HMO to improve their "earnings," and that's charging consumers more and delivering less.

I started my surveillance. The two targets, mother and son, lived together in a walled-off, multimillion-dollar historical mansion in the Garden District area. It was only a couple of miles from the famous the French Quarter. But it might as well have been on the other side of the planet. Walking the stretch from one to the other was like moving from one world to another. The Quarter, as most called it, is historic, beautiful, and teeming with activity nearly twenty-four hours a day. Most of the time it had an edgy, seedy vibe yet never seemed anywhere near as dangerous as it probably was, as if the danger were part of the fun. I could almost imagine someone saying, "Hey look, that guy got stabbed over there," to which his friend would answer, "Great, let's get another beer."

The Garden District is every bit as historic and beautiful but in a completely different way. Its streets are lined with mansions, many gated, and all impeccably landscaped to accent their grand historic beauty. Both areas had largely escaped the flooding and damage of Hurricane Katrina, but neither fully escaped the ensuing post-storm chaos and power outages. The Quarter suffered some looting and vandalism but not the Garden District. The residents had deployed hundreds of armed private security guards, all from neighboring areas, to protect their very valuable assets and homes. I was only slightly surprised to learn that power was restored first in the Garden District. Long before the Quarter and much longer before the rest of the city. Let's face it, in America we're not going to let the rich folks sit in the dark too long. Not that most of them were even there. Van Den Shultz and her son had very publicly evacuated days before the storm, as did almost all of the Garden District residents. That was an unaffordable luxury to the rest of the city's residents, many of whom lost their belongings, homes, or lives.

It would not be easy to get these two. The mother was an octogenarian and rarely left the estate. The son traveled frequently between New Orleans and the company headquarters in Palo Alto. He would travel by limousine back and forth to the airport. He would be easy enough if he were the only target. All I would need to do is set up anywhere along the route. This was no Bentley Flying Spur. I could easily shoot through the windows whether the vehicle was moving or not. But that was of no help in getting the woman I had started calling Momma Shithead. She literally never left the house. Popping her through a window was out of the question. There was simply no safe place to set up. I could pretend to be a ninja, jump the walls, kill the security guys, and pop the old lady, but I would most definitely be caught or killed in that scenario or in any attempt like that outside of a video game. I'm not into suicide missions and thankfully neither is Jane. It occurred to me that there should be an amendment to Jane's philosophy that anyone could be killed. Yes, anyone can be killed if you are willing to die doing it. I wasn't.

Jane was fine with being patient, but I was bored and eager to get to my training vacation and hopefully some time with Linda. Hopefully a lot of time with Linda.

Look, if you gotta be stuck somewhere you can do a lot worse than New Orleans. But we were going on three weeks now, and watching drunk people piss and vomit in the street had lost its appeal.

Fortunately, fate and Jane intervened. The SHIT annual shareholders meeting was being held in a convention center near Palo Alto in a few days. The annual SHIT show, as it was called by some of the more colorful Wall Street analysts. Jane was wagering that both mother and son would attend to show that they were in full control of the company. If she was right, that would leave us with two options: I could fly to Palo Alto ahead of them and try to pick them off coming or going to the meeting, or I could hope mother and son went to the airport together in the same limo. I already knew what my dear aunt would choose. She had rented dwellings along the route that I could set up in, one of which had perfect sightlines to an area with a stop sign. That would be enough for me to pop both. But only if she went. Basically, we were depending on the vanity and lust for power of an old woman born with the privilege of lifelong fabulous wealth. She didn't disappoint us. One full stop and two quick shots was the payoff for weeks of waiting. Both baddies were off to the next life, and I was out of New Orleans. I definitely got the better end of the bargain. Jane's law remained true: You could kill anybody. And you didn't have to die in the attempt. The secret ingredient in this recipe is patience.

TWENTY-TWO

There are three interstate highways that basically dead end in New Orleans, and I ended up picking one more or less at random. I had properly informed Jane that the mission had finally been completed. The text read "Done." I didn't get any immediate response from her, so I just got out of town via the first interstate I saw, which was Interstate Ten toward Baton Rouge. It wasn't unusual that she didn't immediately respond, but it still felt weird. For the first time in eight months, there were no marching orders awaiting me.

My instinct kept me traveling north and I ended up stopping for the night in Texarkana, back in the great state of Texas. Jane finally called and as usual got right to the point.

"I suppose you want to go to New York now, right?" And before I could respond, she continued, "Go ahead, John, you've more than earned it." I couldn't have agreed more.

"How long do I have?" I asked. I was a little bit pissed at myself. I realized later that it would have been the perfect time to ask if Linda could come to New Mexico.

"It's exactly fifteen days until your home in New Mexico will be ready for you, and that's when I expect you to be there." She quickly added, "Have a good time, John," and hung up.

It's almost as if she knew I'd ask about Linda and didn't even want me to have the chance. I could always text. But at the moment, I was happy just to know that I was going to New York.

I hadn't thought about New Mexico in a long time. It seemed like forever ago that it had been my home. It was the last place I had stayed in for more than a few weeks. I guess I thought of it as being my home, but I was only now realizing it. But now it dawned on me that it really wasn't my "home" at all. Jane had said that the house would be ready for me in fifteen days. The only thing that could mean was that it was being used for something. Probably as a training ground for someone like me. I don't think I have ever entertained a jealous thought in my life. I don't really comprehend jealousy. Even if Linda were with another man, I wouldn't feel jealous. A little sad that she didn't want me anymore, yes, but not jealous of her being with someone else. But I had a weird feeling about the house in New Mexico. The thought that there was probably someone there now, training as I had trained, somehow destroyed the notion of it being my home. I wondered if my video game was still attached to the TV in the living room. But it wasn't really my TV or even my living room. I would be going back there soon, but I wouldn't be going home.

I had spoken a handful of times with my parents. Even my home with them wasn't the same anymore. They had moved to a small house with a huge yard in a rural area of Wisconsin. My father had now completely retired. For years he had worked for various Department of Defense contractors. This kept him busy and close to the service both physically and emotionally. I knew that this was very common among retired Army "lifers," as they're sometimes called. You were out, technically, but you were still around it. It was an emotional tether that was very durable. Even now they had still stayed close to an Army base.

My father had bought for my mother what she had always wanted. That was the little house with a ton of land for her to tend to, garden, and grow things. But only twenty miles or so from Fort McCoy was a vast military training facility that was technically part of the Army but provided training for all branches of the service.

I knew the area fairly well. Our family had been stationed there for almost two years when I was in my mid-teens. I first learned to drive in the rural areas north of Fort McCoy where my parents now lived.

I was still driving to Linda in New York, but I had all but decided that I would go to see my parents before heading back to New Mexico. It was no doubt some form of yearning for home that would be automatic in a normal person but almost completely out of character for me.

"You're not a fucken robot," said Kate in response when I brought the subject up. "Even people like you feel things." That was her standard way of not ever directly calling me a sociopath, even knowing full well that I quite neatly fit the profile. She didn't like any generalized statements. "Everybody is different," she would say.

I always felt like she danced around the word because she believed I might be offended by it. The truth was that I couldn't give two shits, and she should probably know as much. But if she wanted to be polite, that was OK too. The bottom line was that she agreed it was a perfect time to see my parents. I'd be lying if I said I missed them. I know that sounds terrible to say, but it's the truth. The only person I have ever really "missed" is Linda. It doesn't mean that I don't care about them or respect them or even love them in my own way. But no, I didn't miss them. I know they missed me though. And that alone was more than enough reason to drive all the way around the Great Lakes to go see them.

Jane didn't protest when I told her of my plans. "You know

where you're supposed to be and when. Whatever you do in between is fine with me." Then she added, "But do me a favor. Try not to kill anybody along the way, and I'm not kidding. The Silencer is still a thing on social media and, believe it or not, because of some of these assholes, your trail is not completely cold. So don't leave any corpses along the way back to New Mexico. Just get there clean, please."

The only thing surprising from that speech was her use of the word "please," which meant that she was very, very serious. Yes, polite equals deadly serious in AJ speak.

I was aware of the weird sort of fame The Silencer had achieved in the world of social media. The only thing that I found surprising is that, for all anyone really knew, I had only killed that one asshole on Fort Lauderdale Beach. There were three different videos of the event that were still circulating, each of which had been viewed at least forty million times. From that single shooting, people were blaming me virtually every time some loudmouth got shot. Yes, there were a few occasions where they linked me to stuff I was actually responsible for, but nine out of ten were just complete nonsense and the stuff of conspiracy theories. It did actually piss me off in a weird way, not because I was accused of being a wanton murderer. Of course, I am a murderer, but not a wanton one. No, it was my sense of professionalism that felt attacked when I was accused of such sloppy, haphazard, and unprofessional work. I could only imagine how the world would react if they knew my true body count. Come to think of it, even I didn't know my true body count—I had lost track. I had come to think of my career as a series of long drives followed by short stays. The work itself was a relatively small amount of my time. In a strange way, I almost thought of myself as a professional driver. I had logged tens of thousands of miles without a single traffic stop, speeding ticket, fender bender, or accident.

Linda welcomed me to New York with a meal she prepared

herself. I think she may have lacked confidence in her cooking skills because she the meal to me completely naked, other than a small loosely tied apron. The idea being that even if I did not enjoy the meal, the presentation would certainly win me over. She was right inasmuch as I would have enjoyed a baked shoe if she served it to me in that manner. She was wrong about her own presumed skills as a chef. She was definitely better than she thought she was, or perhaps she was just better than she'd let on. Either way it was all good. To me the effort was enough. Sometimes it really is the thought that counts. But the food certainly wasn't bad, and her method of serving dessert was quite memorable. I will say only that it wasn't served in the dining room and involved whipped cream.

I figured that we had about a week to spend together. That would leave me enough time to spend a couple of days with my parents in Wisconsin and make it back to New Mexico on schedule. I had decided not to ask Jane about Linda coming to New Mexico. At least not yet. I would wait until I was back at the house and look for gaps or downtimes from my training and then ask if it was possible to bring her in. As well as I knew her, it was still impossible to predict what Jane might rule on the subject. She might very well consider it completely out of bounds. After all it was a government-owned training facility that Jane would consider off limits to any "civilian." But it was also possible she'd surprise me and allow it under certain conditions. It wasn't even a hundred percent certain that Linda would want to come to Bumfuck, New Mexico. Either way I would wait until I was back there to find out.

I only got to spend the first night I was there with Linda in her apartment. Her roommates returned the next day. I took a place in Brooklyn for the rest of my stay and two of us spent the rest of the time there. Four of the days she had to work, so during those days I took to hanging in and around the coffee shop. I went for my runs in Central Park and even a couple of times through the streets of Brooklyn. As the days went by, I almost started to feel like a New Yorker.

Our time together was as comfortable as ever. By comfortable, I mean that it always seemed natural for us to be together. Even if that meant doing nothing. We would watch movies and take turns picking which one. I could feel her gaze on me throughout *Forrest Gump*, her all-time favorite movie. I had never seen it and it really was good. I felt as if I had just passed yet another test when she was assured that I did indeed like it. I was almost as curious to see her reaction to *The Princess Bride* and *The Fifth Element*. Both were old movies that were among my favorites. And she liked them. But as usual, she knew me better than I knew her. She was sure, and correctly so, that I had really enjoyed *Forrest Gump*. I think she liked my movie choices, but I could never be sure that she wasn't just indulging me. But that's OK too. Probably for the same reason, she had enjoyed experiencing my indifference to my first Broadway show. She cared enough about me to pretend to enjoy them even if she didn't, and that was more than enough.

As our time together grew short, I began to play with the idea of revealing part of the areas of my life that were, with good reason, closed off from her. The night before I was due to leave seemed like the right time. We had Chinese food delivered and again sat across from each other at our table for two.

"There are some things I want to tell you . . ." I said, trailing off, ". . . about myself, what I do." I realized in that moment that what I was really doing was revealing enough to make the house in New Mexico make sense to her if I were ever able to bring her there.

"It's about time, John, don't you think?" The way she spoke felt as if these revelations were more for my benefit than hers.

"I'm not a trust-fund kid," I continued. "I have a job, Linda, it's just not a normal one. I do some work for the government, surveillance assignments mostly."

In my mind, this was about as honest as I could possibly be. If I just added, "And I kill the bad people," she would then honestly know my entire career. I didn't add that. Instead, I continued with, "Baby, I wish that I never lied to you, but like everyone else in the world I have a boss. And part of doing my job is making sure no one ever knows I'm doing it . . ." I trailed off again, waiting for some type of reaction.

There wasn't much of one. I don't know what I was expecting but this wasn't it. She just went on eating and paused for a moment to ask me to open a packet of soy sauce for her. The Chinese takeout had come with about ten of those annoying little packets of soy sauce that are almost impossible to open without spilling at least some of it.

"So you're some kind of super-secret agent spy guy?" she asked playfully at the exact moment that the packet tore open and sprayed a dotted line of black soy sauce across my white shirt.

We both laughed as I handed her the now almost empty packet. She did put the remaining two molecules of soy sauce on her rice and then reached for another packet. She somehow opened it flawlessly.

"I hope that made you feel better, John. But honestly, the only thing I care about is you and me. I know you well enough to know that you would never intentionally hurt me, even if that means you lied. I also know that I have your balls tucked neatly away in my purse, right next to my cute little Glock." I just sat in awe of this woman as she continued, "I already know that if you had a choice in the matter, you would be with me all of the time. So, if you aren't with me, there has to be a pretty damn good reason. This spy shit is as good a reason as any. If it makes you feel any better, I will say out loud what you probably already know. I choose to be with you, as much or as little as life permits. I choose you."

I have, to this point anyway, led an incredibly lucky, almost charmed life. That exact moment was the high point. She was right, of course. She did have my balls safely tucked away. But at the risk of being coarse, she wanted me to know that I had her heart safely tucked away as well.

"Just do your best not to lie to me" were her final words on the subject.

Getting that out of the way was quite freeing. We spent our last night together talking. Well, mostly talking. There was also a fair bit of "laying all over" each other. But I was now free to tell her more about myself. My parents, family, and upbringing as an Army brat. I did leave out AJ. But pretty much everything else was now fair game. It felt good to know that I was now down to just one lie. Granted, it was a big one. As close as we now were, I still could not reveal my life as The Silencer. Linda had also seen the social media frenzy that had sprung up from that day on the beach. She had a special interest in it because she was there, on the beach, when it actually happened. We, in fact, had watched one of the online videos together, marveling at the fact that we had been so close to an event that had been seen across the globe. Of course, I had a slightly different perspective on the matter.

For the first time I was able to tell my girlfriend what I was doing when I left. I was going to see my parents in Wisconsin.

TWENTY-THREE

I hadn't heard a single word from either Kate or Jane the entire time I was in New York. Again, an act of kindness from the other women in my life. It was a sixteen-hour drive to my parents which for me is practically next door. I had logged so many driving miles that a sixteen hours just didn't seem like that much. Nevertheless, I divided it into two days.

I didn't want to start keeping any more secrets. I had told Linda a great deal more about who I was. I wanted to make sure both of the other women in my life were informed. Knowing them, they would probably figure it out anyway, so why waste energy by trying. So I started by calling Kate, thinking she would probably be more receptive to the idea, yet I was surprised by her response to my carefully worded confession. "Are you sure that was wise, John? More importantly, do you think Jane will think it was wise?"

I wasn't ready for that kind of response and explained. "Whether it's wise or not, I still think it was the right thing to do. She is hopefully going to be part of my life for a long time and, trust me on this, she is far from stupid. I think this way there will be far fewer questions rather than more." This was probably true, but I was really just testing it out with Kate to see how it might later go over with Jane.

"That may be true, John, and it doesn't bother me, but be honest with yourself about why you told her. You did it because you wanted to. Why? Because you wanted to be even closer to her and you don't want to lie to her any more than you have to. I totally get it, and it may even have been the right thing to do, but don't bother bullshitting me or your aunt about why you did it because we both know better and, truthfully, so do you."

You would think that I would have learned by this point that the women of my life were always way ahead of me. This time they were so far ahead that I briefly thought I was.

She added, "I'm sure you're going to tell Jane, so I don't have to remind you that, if you don't tell her, I would be obligated to."

I did already know that and responded listlessly, "Yeah, I know. I might as well bite the bullet."

She ended the call with some reassurance. "It'll be fine, John. Just don't bother with any excuses, just tell her the truth. You told Linda because you wanted to and leave it at that. She won't be thrilled, but she will understand."

I saved Kate the trouble and called Jane myself. She answered the phone with, "It's fine, John."

Now I was confused. "What's fine?" I asked.

"Whatever it is that you are about to tell me that you are sure I won't like, it's fine." Turns out she didn't already know and was just guessing, and I had pretty much just walked into it. I did what Kate said to do. I said right away that I gave Linda information about my life because we had been together for a while, and I wanted to lie to her as little as possible.

"Exactly how much did you tell her?" was Jane's first question.

"Pretty much everything except the money shot," I replied, thinking that was a particularly clever way to say it.

"That's funny, John. Or rather it would be funny if the person you were making porno jokes to wasn't your aunt."

We both laughed. It occurred to me that it might have been the first time we had made each other laugh. It's not that our conversations were dour or unpleasant. It was just that our subject matter usually wasn't something to joke about. She made it clear that she didn't approve and that I should have asked her first. Before taking such a big step with real potential risk. And make no mistake, there was potential risk. Linda was amazing. But what if something went wrong and our relationship broke up. That would leave us with some very difficult decisions, so there was no doubt risk. But, somehow, Jane understood. Soon our conversation turned to my destination.

"I haven't seen your folks since we first started," she said. "Please tell them I said hi. I'm so happy for your mom, she finally got what she always wanted." She was talking about the little house with the big garden. It was the first time in recent memory that we talked about our family. It was nice.

Middle-of-nowhere Wisconsin was pretty much the same as I remembered from ten years earlier. My parents' "new" house was exactly as described. It was a very small, very old house on a very big lot. The land was at least an acre, and the house was indeed small. Probably no more than eight or nine hundred square feet. But it did have two bedrooms, and the second contained all the things I had left behind when I started life in Jane's world. My bed, my dresser, and my nightstand were all there and arranged exactly as they had been in my old bedroom but with a little less space around them. Even most of the clothes I'd left behind were carefully hung in the closet and neatly folded in the drawers. Their little boy may have left them, but they had never left their little boy. I tried on a few things just to see how they fit. I admit to feeling some slight satisfaction that they fit almost exactly the way they always had. I'd had no occasion to weigh myself since New Mexico, but I was now certain that my weight was probably the same as it had been then. It had been more than twenty months since I had last seen my parents in person, but they had barely changed. My dad carried at most five extra pounds, but my mom was actually thinner than I remembered and definitely tanner. It must have been all that work in her beautiful garden.

It wasn't my thing, but I could see the artistry of taking an area of crabgrass and rock and slowly molding it into a beautiful landscape of color, tranquility, and productivity. Our first dinner together included tomatoes that she had grown herself. They were the most delicious I had ever tasted. And since you know me, you know that I mean it. I lack any of the sensitivity it takes to tell my mother they were good if they weren't. I was smart enough to not tell her they sucked if they had sucked, but they were delicious. Much better than anything you could buy in a supermarket. I complimented my mom on her handiwork and made a mental note to myself to research why a home-grown tomato tasted so much better than store-bought. It turns out that it was yet another corporate rabbit hole. But in the moment, I was happy because my mom was happy and, in his own way, so was my old man.

"She's out there ten hours a day at least," my father said with a mix of pride and feigned annoyance. "I drag my ass out there and help her from time to time, but she runs the show. Lucky for her, she has a man who is quite accustomed to following orders." He laughed. We all did. In that small window of time, we were a happy family, together again.

"Dad, when it comes to women, I have learned exactly who is really in charge."

My mom shared a wide smile and asked, "You only just figured that out? I thought I taught you that long ago. But you aren't supposed to tell anybody," she whispered conspiratorially. "You boys do so much better when we let you think that you are in charge."

I may not have really understood that when I left home. But I certainly do now. Any moron who still believes that women are the weaker sex is probably named Bob and is right now slamming tequilas and saying stupid things in that shithole back in New Mexico. I remembered something I had read during one of the rare times I had chosen to read a novel rather than nonfiction. In the chaos of post-World War II Europe, people were still dying from land mines that had been planted during the war. The character in the novel commented that there was no way to know which army had planted the devices. But there was no doubt about which gender had done so. The speaker was certain that only a man would seed such a device that would maim and kill so indiscriminately. My aunt, who is also my boss, has ordered the deaths of an untold number of people, yet I could still agree with the sentiment of that fictional character.

The next morning, my mom enlisted me in what she called her "Garden Army." I was completely clueless and probably not much help, but that wasn't really the point. We got to spend some time together, and my mom got to show off her work. And it really was impressive. She was growing at least two dozen different herbs, vegetables, and fruits. All of it was neatly sectioned and manicured. Even with all of that, she was still using less than a quarter of the land she had at her disposal. I imagined coming back a year later and finding another whole section created by my mom. I can't say that gardening with her had awakened in me some strong desire to someday do the same, but it did make me realize that there was a lot to it. There was a lot to know, a lot to learn, and a lot to admire when you see somebody working so well and so hard at something they love. The takeaway for me was that not all lessons are spoken aloud and not all learning comes from a book.

As I started my drive south, I was glad I had made the trip to see my parents. This was the first time in a long time that I had some time to really think about some of the events, the crazy amount of driving, and some of the ideas that were still pretty new to me. Some of those ideas had been literally shoe-horned into me by Jane and Kate. That was fine, as long as it was truth. When I started thinking about truth was the first time that I fully understood that I, and all of us, spend our entire lives being lied to virtually every minute of the day. It was no wonder that so many otherwise normal people have become so completely detached from reality. We have talked a lot about how the world has made so many of us ridiculously addicted to trying to attract any kind of attention to themselves. Truth, it seems to me, is a corollary of that concept. We have been lied to so many times that we don't know the truth when we see it. I am a sociopath. One of the few good things about being a sociopath is that we can see the truth when it is shown to us. I doubt you would find even a single Flat Earther that is also a sociopath, but that's not true of the "normal" among us. And they have been lied to about things large and small from the moment they first realized that Daddy's face was still there whenever he played a game of peekaboo with them. Every radio and TV commercial is a lie of many varieties. Every polit-ical commercial or speech is at best misleading and more commonly these days all lies. When Jitstain Joe, owner of Jitstain Joes Dodge Chrysler Jeep goes on TV. He says that his dealership exists to serve you and sell you the best car at the best price. Jitstain Joe might actually believe it, but Jitstain Joe is lying. His business, like every business on the planet, exists to create revenue. His business exists so that Joe can have a forty-foot yacht that he doesn't know how to sail. His business exists so that his wife, who is twenty-three years his junior, can afford to have toxins injected into her face that make her nose and lips pinched to the point that her expression is that of someone who is always smelling shit. I know this because she's always in his commercials, standing next to Jitstain Joe, trying to sell whatever bullshit he's selling. Her face frozen in a bizarre, clown like smirk of discomfort. As if she can smell the shit of Joe's proximity. Joe's actual purpose is to pry as much money out of you as possible. And anyone who has ever been to any car dealership knows that the number of lies you hear from them on TV is dwarfed by the lies you hear once you have crossed their threshold.

I could easily have spent the rest of that day's drive thinking of the hundreds of ways we are all lied to on a daily basis. But one particularly spectacular display of douchebaggery kept popping in and out of my head. Florida Power and Light is the only electricity supplier for more than eleven million people in Florida. That means the vast majority of people have no choice about who they buy power from. If you want to make toast in Florida, you have two choices: pay FPL all the money they want or try to make toast with a blow torch while standing in a dark, hot room. But that's not even close to the worst part. FPL spends millions of their victim's money on advertising just to tell their victims how wonderful they are.

Seriously, when I was in Fort Lauderdale, I saw what seemed like a thousand commercials telling me how great FPL is. How many loyal, wholesome, patriotic, and gritty Floridians they employ and how hard they are working to stop climate change by using solar power. There was just one small problem: FPL actually uses almost no solar energy. Just enough to put on a show. They had also spent millions of their victims' dollars lobbying in four straight elections against anyone using solar power, including and especially their customers. They used their monopoly power and money literally stolen from Floridians to prevent Floridians from breaking free from their monopoly. All of this in the Sunshine State, a place so suitable for solar power that it could probably generate enough power without producing more climate-destroying carbon. This was the most astounding display of corruption and hypocrisy. The one thing it most definitely is not, is free market capitalism. It is corruption, plain and simple. And it harms every single person in the state. If I could talk Jane into it, which I most certainly could not, I would gladly spend the rest of my career popping every one of these corporate thieves and every one of the corrupt politicians on their payroll.

That was on my mind as I worked my way south toward New Mexico.

Not far out of my way was that world capital of corruption known as Bentonville, Arkansas. I'm not sure why I wanted to stop there, but it most certainly was not my purpose to "go rogue" and start popping CRAPpers against the explicit instructions of AJ.

As expected, she was not amused. "What the fuck are you doing there, John?" she asked.

I wasn't trying to hide anything. I know full well that Jane always knows my whereabouts. I had a couple of days until I was due in New Mexico. I wanted to take a look around CRAP headquarters, hoping that the information would be helpful in some future mission. But Jane was having none of it.

"You want to spend your time jerking off, then go ahead and do it. But as I've told you fifty-seven times and counting, we are not ready to take them on. Just get to New Mexico on time." And she hung up.

That was fair enough. I spent that day and the next watching the comings and goings of the barely human lowlifes that were destroying capitalism, destroying the value of hard work, and destroying the planet itself. Nothing much unusual happened until early that evening. Two lobbyists were leaving CRAP headquarters around dinnertime. Accompanying this pair of assholes was an old "friend," the Saudi bodyguard I had failed to kill when I had the chance. To say that this caused me some confusion would be similar to saying that the Titanic had suffered a slight boating mishap. In my world, this changed everything.

I called Jane and, for once, I didn't let her get the first or last words.

"What the fuck is going on?" I asked in a way that sounded more like a demanding growl.

I don't think she knew what I was so upset about, so she asked, "What happened?"

"Remember that Saudi bodyguard? You might recall that he's still alive because I didn't fill this scumbag with bullet holes. Well, he's here and protecting at least two CRAPpers that I know of. I'm sure he's doing it in his usual ludicrously incompetent way, but what the fuck is going on? Whose side are we on anyway?"

These might be the only words I ever said to my aunt that she didn't already know were coming. She waited what seemed like a very long time before answering. And when she did get around to answering, it was with a mix of kindness and menace that only a true sociopath can comprehend. "Look, John, there is a lot going on that you can't possibly understand. There is even some stuff that even I can't even understand. But I want you to understand one thing. You are to get in your car right now and get to New Mexico. Not in an hour, not after dinner, now, please!"

I knew what that meant. She couldn't explain to me how this guy who should already have been dead was here and helping some of the worst people on planet Earth. The fact that she added "please" was of particular concern. I knew it meant we were on dangerous ground. But I was inflated with righteous anger and, yeah, probably some god-like delusion that I was going to fix the world singlehandedly.

That led to my extremely stupid response, "I will leave tomorrow, or maybe even the next day, and still make it to New Mexico on time just as you ordered."

"John, I suggest that you choose your next words very, very carefully. Will you leave Bentonville right now?"

I chose to ignore the tone of her question and answered, "I will be in New Mexico at the agreed-upon time."

Jane answered with a curt "I see" and hung up.

Dammit! I had certainly got the first words, but I didn't get the last word. And I finished that conversation feeling uneasy. Much more than ever before.

I spent the rest of that evening till early the next morning watching my Saudi friend, and it became clear that he was in the employ of CRAP. If I'm being honest with myself, I probably would've popped that guy if I could have. But I was traveling clean and had no weapons on hand. Looking back now, it was probably a good thing that I didn't.

I still fully intended to get back to New Mexico as promised, just not quite yet. I could leave the next morning and still have plenty of time to make it.

I spent most of that day watching the Saudi and some others. Late in the afternoon, I returned to my apartment and found an unwelcome surprise. Already in my apartment were two uniformed police officers. I found out later that they were the only two officers in this extremely small town just a few miles from Bentonville proper. Before I got a chance to ask, the two white, and quite burly, officers declared me under arrest. I offered no resistance. How could I? I was unarmed and that moment not much more than the goofy young punk I appeared to be. They handcuffed me and placed me in the back of their police cruiser. An ancient vehicle they may well have borrowed from the set of *The Andy Griffith Show*.

Yes, there was Plexiglas between me in the back and them in the front seat. But that didn't stop me from hearing every word the two putzes said to each other. I hadn't yet asked them why I was being arrested, but it turns out it didn't matter because they didn't know either.

"I don't know why Langley is making such a big deal about this kid."

I could hear them speaking to each other with perfect clarity. Langley, of course, refers to the CIA, whose headquarters were in Langley, Virginia. His partner snorted with mocking laughter.

"I love the way you say Langley, as if the CIA is calling you for shit every other day. I don't know what their problem is with this kid, but if they say to hold him, we hold him. We don't need to give them any reason to come poking around down here. They can come and get him tomorrow morning and then hopefully go away."

These two geniuses were talking like I wasn't even there. Whatever they were talking about wasn't on the up and up, but they didn't seem to care if I heard them. Or maybe they were just stupid enough to think I couldn't hear them through that thin piece of Plexiglas. For a brief moment, I thought I might be getting popped, since they didn't seem to know or care that I could hear them. But then I remembered that they were under orders to hold me until tomorrow morning for the CIA. Well, it looked like I was heading in the Andy Griffith car to the Andy Griffith jail.

At least I wasn't getting popped. For the moment that was good enough for me.

TWENTY FOUR

y jailers were not rude to me nor rough on me. In fact, they were pretty much just indifferent to me. As if I were a package delivered to the wrong address and they were eagerly awaiting the rightful owners to come pick it up. They didn't even get around to booking me or taking my mugshot.

A little after midnight, the fatter of the two wandered in with two big bags of McDonald's and a couple of Cokes.

"You hungry?" he asked. "Who knows when they're coming to get you, so you might as well eat something."

Once I had agreed, he unlocked the cell with the kind of old-school steel key that itself could have been a prop from *The Andy Griffith Show*. Obviously, he had no fear of me as he simply unlocked the gate long enough to hand me the burger, fries, and Coke.

Soon it was clear that his kindness was not without motive. For a few minutes we ate in silence, me in my cell and him at a desk just a few feet way.

"So what do you suppose they want you for?" he asked in an embarrassingly bad attempt to sound casual about it.

This rekindled in me the notion that these two fucks might pop me. From what I heard, I knew that they were involved in some kind of shit. Shit that was serious enough for them to worry about the officials coming to pick me up. I could almost hear them making the calculation in their heads. Was CIA involvement with me just a fluke or did it have something to do with whatever shenanigans they were up to? Would it be safer for them to stage my death in my cell, or just hope that I had nothing to do with anything they were afraid of being found out about?

I didn't have to consider the question for long. The other officer walked into the room. He was closely followed by another man I couldn't see from where I was sitting. I heard a single shot that caused the standing officer to crumple to the floor, dead of a single shot to the back of his head. The other officer jumped to his feet, reaching clumsily for his holstered weapon. He didn't have a chance. The man shot him just above his nose. He, too, crumpled quickly to the ground. Dead.

I was in some kind of shock myself. I have done way more than my own share of killing, but it was never this close, this real. My shock only deepened when I realized who the man was who had killed the two cops. It was the Saudi I myself had spared. He could only be here for one reason, or so I thought. I once again prepared myself for the blackness of death. But again, it did not come.

"Hurry up," he said again with his thick accent. "Unless you'd rather stay here?" he asked, quite rhetorically. By then he had grabbed the key from the dead guard and unlocked the cell. I was starting to get my wits about me and followed him quickly out the door, into a small empty room, and then out onto the darkened street.

He gestured to a car at the curb. It was my own black SUV. I started to open the driver's side door of the car when he stopped me.

"Other side," he said, gesturing to me with the handgun that he still held, pointed at me. I walked quickly to the other side and was about to open the door when he stopped me. "Hey," he said, "I'd say this makes us even." He holstered the weapon and walked away before I could reply.

I still didn't know why, but I jumped in the passenger side of my car as I had been instructed to at gun point.

"Hi, baby," said Linda, sitting in the driver's seat, acting as if this were all perfectly normal.

I realized I had not the slightest fucken concept of what normal actually was anymore. If I'd taken the time to count them, I had somewhere in the range of a thousand questions that I could've asked in that moment. But Linda was already driving us away and that helped me to narrow things down a little.

So I settled on "Where are we going?"

She smiled and turned to glance at me, but for just a moment. "Where do you think we're going?" she asked with that now familiar playful lilt to her voice.

I didn't answer for a while, and the more she drove the more obvious the answer became. "New Mexico?" I finally ventured. Her ever so slight nod opened up about ten thousand more questions, not a single one I wanted to ask right now. But there was one that I knew I wouldn't have to ask because the answer was already blindingly obvious. There weren't two women in my life who could effortlessly manipulate me. There were three. The meaning of the third one would take the combined efforts of every psychiatrist in the known universe to figure out. Despite the fact that I am a sociopath, or perhaps because of it, I was oddly and perfectly content to sit next to this woman and follow here where she was leading. She seemed to sense that and did not at all attempt to answer any of the questions that would have to be answered in the coming days.

For now, at least, I was alive, safe, and in the company of the person that I most wanted to be with. That was enough. For now.

TWENTY-FIVE

The miles went by, and night soon turned into dawn. Linda was hungry, so we found a place to eat near the interstate. The truth was I was hungry too. I had never quite eaten my burger before my Saudi friend had relieved my captors of their corporeal existence. We took our time but spoke very little. There just wasn't a lot to talk about that wouldn't lead into much bigger questions that I just didn't want to know the answers to yet.

The same continued when we got back on the road. After a while I turned on the radio. Over the next couple of hours, I heard a couple news reports that I found to be of some interest.

The Upstate New York town of Allset was racked by a massive explosion early this morning. The blast was so powerful that it reduced the building to little more than a pile of rubble. Local authorities announced that there were no fatalities resulting from the blast, though there were several minor injuries to firefighters and rescue workers dispatched to the scene. The building was the lone laboratory of a Department of Defense contractor called Geneworks. Authorities have so far offered no theories as to the cause of the blast.

In other news, Grant Pearson, Jr., the president and CEO of

Surety Health Insurance Technology was found dead today at his winter home in Aspen, Colorado. Authorities are still investigating but have disclosed that he died of a single gunshot wound to the head. He is the fourth chief executive of the massive HMO to have died under mysterious circumstances in the last six months.

"How about a little music?" said Linda as she began twisting the dial. But not before offering me a knowing glance. There was no doubt that she knew what those radio reports meant. Probably even better than I did. For some reason, I felt the need to make a little conversation, so I chose what I thought would be the most innocuous subject I could think of.

"I didn't even know you could drive," I said to Linda. "As far as I know you never needed a car in New York."

"Oh, I have a license," she answered happily. "You never know when it might come in handy." She reached in her purse and handed me her license. It was a New Mexico license. It had her picture and bore the name Linda Davidson Frum. She looked over at my surprised face and announced, "Congratulations, honey, we're married!"

I hadn't the slightest idea how to answer that revelation and Linda somehow sensed that enough was enough. There were only so many things that a person could absorb at one time. And she knew full well that I had received more than enough surprises for one day.

I took over the driving and the two of us just sat side by side, watching as the vast blues, reds, and golds of the sunrise played out before our eyes.

There were exactly two things that I was certain about. The first was that the things that I know and the things that I think I know are completely different. The second was that there was still a great deal of work to be done. It seems that Jane had decided, at least for now, that I would still be one of the people to do that work.

ABOUT THE AUTHOR

David Litvin has spent most of his adult life in two worlds. The first was in the Basque sport of Jai Alai. He was the U.S National Amateur Jai-Alai champion in 1990. He played jai alai in the Campeonato De Mundial (World Championship) in Havana, Cuba, as part of the Pan American Games. As a representative of the United States, a fourth-place finish earned the U.S. a berth in the 1992 Olympic Games in Barcelona, Spain. Later, his attention turned to the world of poker where he was a profitable, professional player and later a poker dealer, poker tournament director, and poker room director.

His previous work is a musical stage play about the world of high stakes poker, *All In: The Poker Musical,* which featured original songs by Grammy award winner Vini Poncia.

He tries to keep his needs simple and his masters few.

THE AUTHOR MAY BE REACHED AT:
DLKOSMO@GMAIL.COM OR
DAVIDLITVIN.COM

ALSO BY DAVID L. LITVIN

The Monochrome Solution

Frum God: The Mostly True Adventures of a Modern Day Messiah

All In: The Poker Musical